To Susan,

THE TANGLEVILLE CHRONICLES

Does Father Know Best?

Many thanks for your contribution to this novel. Very much appreciated!

Donald H. Hull

Blessings,

Don

 FriesenPress

Suite 300 - 990 Fort St
Victoria, BC, V8V 3K2
Canada

www.friesenpress.com

Copyright © 2019 by Donald H. Hull
First Edition — 2019

All rights reserved.

No part of this publication may be reproduced in any form, or by any means, electronic or mechanical, including photocopying, recording, or any information browsing, storage, or retrieval system, without permission in writing from FriesenPress.

ISBN
978-1-5255-5746-0 (Hardcover)
978-1-5255-5747-7 (Paperback)
978-1-5255-5748-4 (eBook)

1. FICTION, CHRISTIAN, CONTEMPORARY

Distributed to the trade by The Ingram Book Company

Reviews

The final book of the *Tangleville* trilogy puts forth a compelling question: Does Father know best? We are continuously bombarded with competing truth claims. Which voice should we listen to? Which voice should we believe? There are far too many voices feeding compounding doubts and unanswered questions and turning people back to God is becoming increasingly difficult. It is here that The Rev. Dr. Barclay Steadmore finds his voice to proclaim anew, traditional biblical understanding.

Not only does Barclay step out, he steps up to defend the faith, taking head on some of the more controversial social issues of our day. When most people would rather stand on the sidelines, in the name of tolerance, Barclay confidently responds. He outlines clear viewpoints that align with God's Word and biblical morality. Whether believer or unbeliever, the reader is left to answer: Does Father know best? Barclay's compelling insights will most certainly promote a heightened awareness and introspection on several moral and ethical topics challenging Christians today. Rather than comfortable or complacent, Christians are called to boldly expose biblical truths and unite believers. Like Barclay, may we all be fully open to the Spirit's promptings, and embody the strength and courage to respond to the calling.

Dr. Susan Munro, COO, Munro & Associates, Inc.

Be ready to be pulled into this story—this is the most fast-paced and controversial of Dr. Don Hull's trilogy. The author very adeptly develops the characters of The Rev. Canon Dr. Barclay Steadmore and his compatriots to "… arouse a complacent culture …" (52). This page-turner book is insightful, honest, humorous, contemporary, and relevant for anyone who wishes to explore and be challenged by spiritual issues—regardless of your religious perspective. Be prepared for a surprise and suspense-filled finale that guarantees you won't want to put the book down!

Randall G. Hart, B.SC.(For), RPF (Ret), CBC (Ret)

Donald Hull has done it again! In the third book and final edition of the *Tangleville* trilogy, he has found yet another forum for The Rev. Dr. Barclay Steadmore to express his opinions and views as a devout Christian in today's secular society. While you may not agree with all of those views, you can respect the passion and conviction with which they are expressed within the story set out in *Does Father Know Best?*

Terry Pearce, B.A., LL.B., Municipal Prosecutor

Foreword

IN the Spring of 2016 we were invited to participate in a journey that began in a sleepy little town called Tangleville. This town was not dissimilar to a lot of small towns that dot the landscape of North America. As a place which was described as "Just About Any Town Anywhere," it had the typical strengths that come from strong community connections where most folk know one another by name. Conversely, it also exhibited the challenges that can sometimes arise from those same close ties which bind individuals to their friends and neighbours. In towns like this, one's actions and words can start something of a ripple effect that sees the impact spread out in ever wider circles throughout the whole community.

There is no question that this describes the effect of the words and actions of our protagonist in this literary journey, The Rev. Canon Dr. Barclay Steadmore. On this sojourn with Dr. Steadmore, we have seen how his thoughtful and faithful challenge against the secular gospel of today's culture changed the lives of everyone he encountered as he encouraged them to look a little deeper at the meaning of life. In the sequel to the first book, *Untangling Tangleville*, Dr. Steadmore took a new challenge to Tangleville's numerous Christian communities, as he pushed them to consider what impact a united witness to the gospel of Christ might have. In each step of this journey, readers have been challenged to consider their own convictions and what tangible steps they can take as they strive to be faithful to their own call to follow Jesus Christ.

My own journey with our author, The Rev. Canon Dr. Donald Hull, began many years ago on a retreat. It was in the early autumn of 1995 that I first met him as he led a retreat for transitional deacons preparing for ordination to the Anglican priesthood. I came to an understanding during the course of that prayerful time that Don had an unrelenting and passionate dedication to promoting the traditional, orthodox Christian faith as it has been lived out in the lives of everyday saints for centuries. Neither of us could have known then that some eleven years later I would take over as his successor as the Rector of Church of the Ascension and our journey of faith together, working alongside one another for the sake of the gospel, would continue in new and profound ways.

It is with that same dedication and passion that Dr. Hull brings us this third and final book in the *Tangleville* series. We continue journeying with Dr. Steadmore in this story as he tackles some of the most pressing issues that face our society from the Christian perspective. As each of the books in this series has done, it will undoubtedly challenge and push you, the reader, to consider what it is you believe and where it is you stand in relation to the modern tug-of-war between matters of faith and secular society's position. This is a book which invites its readers into a process of deliberation which will see very few on the sidelines or sitting on the fence by its end, and perhaps that is exactly the point!

As this literary journey we were invited to join draws to an end, I am sure that Dr. Hull intends that you recognize that this story is one whose impact continues to be played out in the lives of faithful Christians everywhere, every day. The challenges that confronted Dr. Steadmore as he sought to be faithful to the Christian gospel have not gone away. So the story goes on, the journey continues as Christians in every town, everywhere, continue their faithful pilgrimage toward the Kingdom of God that Jesus came to proclaim.

The Rev. Canon Lance S. Smith, B.A., M.Div.,
Rector, Church of the Ascension, Windsor, ON

*To my spouse Faye, and the
Mullins, Livermore, and Armstrong families:
You are gifts from God!*

Acknowledgements

THIS final novel, the third in the Tangleville series, would not have been possible without the assistance of two people who contributed to its creation:

Gillian Matthewman spent many hours typing the manuscript, which was written entirely in longhand. She is a master in untangling my almost impossible style of penmanship. She caught many situations where rewriting was necessary. Thank-you Gillian!

To Faye, my spouse and proofreader, I am deeply grateful. Her insistence on clarity and spelling, sentence structure, and punctuation was responsible for serious changes from the original manuscript.

* * *

Scripture quotations are from the New Revised Standard Version Bible, copyright 1989, the Division of Christian Education of the National Council of the Churches of Christ in the United States of America. Used by permission. All rights reserved.

Introduction

THE past viewed and analyzed through the rear view mirror of life, most certainly will influence discussions to become history in the future.

> *"Man is a history-making creature, who can neither repeat his past nor leave it behind."*
> W.H. Auden, The Dyers Hand

Soren Kierkegaard (1813–1855) put it in a way that rational and courageous beings cannot file away in dusty history books:

> *"During the first period of man's life the greatest danger is not to take the risk."*

Influence, history-making individuals, and risk were the themes of the previous two novels:

> *Tangleville, Just About Any Town Anywhere;* and
> *Untangling Tangleville, Stepping Out, Just As Any Town Can*

The publication of those two novels necessitated this final book:

The Tangleville Chronicals

If these first two books have been read, the reader will recall the great changes that had taken place in the lives of Harry Sting, The Rev. Canon Dr. Barclay Steadmore and his supportive spouse Faith. Risk was involved in each of their freewill choices as they determined to follow the challenge of the Holy Spirit. Edith Wharton put it this way:

> "*There are two ways of spreading light:*
> *to be the candle or the mirror that reflects it.*"

All three, Harry and the Steadmores, are examples of those who defied what Elbert Hubbard once said: "*The greatest mistake you can make in life is to be continually fearing that you will make one.*"

This third and final volume of the Tangleville trilogy will confirm what the doxology at the conclusion of the service of the Holy Eucharist states:

> *Glory to God,*
> *whose power working in us,*
> *can do infinitely more*
> *than we can ask or imagine.*
> *Glory to God from generation to generation,*
> *in the Church and in Christ Jesus,*
> *for ever and ever. Amen.*

(The Book of Alternative Services of the Anglican Church of Canada, 214.)

All Christians, especially in this secular age, are called to unite in order to overcome the fear of criticism and stand firm in the building of the Kingdom of God.

Howard Ruff said: "*It wasn't raining when Noah built the ark.*"

The storm clouds of secular society are ever darkening! We each, as followers of Christ, can choose to be the candle or the mirror (or both) that reflects our faith.

You decide: Does Father know best?

Chapter One

THE bedside phone was ringing! Dr. Steadmore glanced over at the digital clock next to the night reading lamp. It was 11:38 p.m. on a Thursday evening in late May.

"Hello, this is Barclay speaking."

"Doctor, I apologize for calling so late, but I wanted you to be the first of my out-of-town friends to receive the news."

"Harry, is everything OK? You sound very animated. You never call this late in the evening!"

"Doctor, I've just won the seat on town council in Ward One. The final votes have been counted and even though it was a squeaker, it is official. I have a new title in Tangleville: Councillor."

"Well, congratulations Harry! Well done! I've felt all along that you would pull it off. When is the official swearing-in ceremony? Faith and I will do our best to be there with you."

"Three weeks from today. Annie wants you and Faith to come a day or two early and spend some time with us. We haven't been together now for months. Can you make it?"

Harry Sting and Barclay could chat for only a few minutes as the press from the radio station AM KNOW, the *Tangleville Mirror*, and the local television station were pressing in for interviews.

"I have got to go, Barclay. Annie sends her love. We will be waiting for your reply to come home to Tangleville. My love to Faith! God bless!"

It was great news! Barclay decided not to wake Faith to give her Harry's good news. That could wait until morning.

Now wide awake himself, his thoughts recounted the incredible transformation that had taken place in Harry's life and his own: his first on-air interview with that then anti-religious talk show host at AM KNOW ... becoming a regular on his show ... the growing friendship between Harry and Annie and Faith and himself. It all seemed to be a miracle, looking back at Harry's religious conversion, baptism, confirmation, and membership at St. Bartholomew's Anglican parish ... culminating with Harry becoming the CEO of The Samaritan Inn ... his appointment as Lay Canon by Bishop Strictman and media director for the Diocese.

There was no doubt that the formation of Tangleville's *Christian Coalition Manifesto* was initially instigated by Harry, even though the Rev. Dr. Angus McLaughlin, minister of St. Andrew's Presbyterian Church, and Father Leo Mahoney of St. Anne's Roman Catholic parish had picked up the ball and guided it into the final published document. With the coalition finally consisting of twelve of Tangleville's major Christian denominations, the unified Christian voice in the town had been a major force in challenging secular affairs. Other surrounding towns were noticing how Tangleville's Christians were prepared to work together while still maintaining their own denominational liturgical practices during Sunday worship. But when it came to a voice in town to protest and unify long-established Christian values in a secular age, the churches spoke with one voice ... a voice that was not to be taken lightly ... especially by town council and official secular fund raising events.

On looking back, it should not have been a surprise to the Christian community when Harry first announced that he was going to toss his hat into the ring to run for town council in Ward One.

Supported financially through fund raising by the Christian community, but primarily through the financial support of his affluent spouse, Annie, Harry's campaign was successful. He won by a close margin of 189 votes more than his closet rival, Chip Graves, CEO of Tangleville's downtown Casino. Certainly Dr. McLaughlin's weekly article in the *Tangleville Mirror*, "The Cleric Speaks," swayed many undecided voters to turn out to the polls and vote for the outspoken Harry.

Of course, the secularists in Tangleville were outraged. Not accustomed to being criticized and opposed by an articulate, vocal consolidated religious voice, readers' articles soon appeared in the *Tangleville Mirror*, expressing fear that the status quo was being usurped by religious organizers. "There must be the separation of church and state" was the common complaint. "We don't want religion shoved down our throats!" "Keep your religious connections within the walls of your churches."

Harry, up until his swearing-in day as town councillor, continued to host his radio show at AM KNOW. Ratings went through the roof following the election as both supporters and opponents duked it out over the air. Harry and Annie both agreed that after taking his seat on town council, he would need to cease being an employee of the station. This was announced during his last half hour segment on Friday of the last week in May. It was a bitter sweet day for Harry ... but new doors were opening. Harry was ready to walk into the future.

* * *

It was nearly two years ago following the Reverend Doctor Barclay Steadmore's retirement from St. Bart's that he and Faith moved from Tangleville to Trinity Harbour. It had been a rectorship of fifteen years in town. Both knew that it would be easier for his successor, Rev. Canon Matthew Hudson, to assume leadership in the parish if he and Faith were not available and considered as competition to Matthew's ministry. Barclay was grateful and honoured that on occasion, he would be invited back as guest preacher at St. Bart's and as a special guest on Harry's show. Whenever in town, they were always the guests of Harry and Annie. Their friendship grew stronger over the years in spite of the fact that they were now separated by 110 miles. Living in a high-rise condo on the water's edge was a delightful way to live out their retirement years together.

However, it had soon become evident to Barclay following his retirement that he was not ready to put down the pen. Writing a weekly sermon had been one of the highlights of being a rector. Scholarly research and keeping up with temporal events in the media always led to timely homilies ... applying Biblical truth to the ever-changing whims and morals of the secular age. Faith knew that her husband needed a challenge to keep his mind active, and to—as she put it to herself—keep him out of her hair, as she continued to adapt to her new life in Trinity Harbour. She was too polite and too loving to use those words. There are times when words need to be measured, restrained, and never uttered.

"Barclay, why don't you write about the life of a rector in a busy parish? Maybe call it 'The Steadmore Chronicles.' How about highlighting some of the amusing events that took place during your ministry? I'm sure that there are lots of people out there who have no idea how and what a priest does on a daily basis."

Barclay thought about it for a few weeks while it was gelling in his mind. So many clergy upon retirement publish a book of homilies which had been preached over past years. But that didn't seem to appeal to him. After all, those sermons were clearly written, and in many cases, out-dated, having at the time addressed pertinent issues of the day. Besides, to publish such a book would only require him to edit his best sermons and after sorting and doing so, then he still would not be generating new ideas … addressing issues which had been for some time percolating in his mind, but never seriously thought through or pursued.

Maybe that was it … to choose subjects, issues, and problems that laity may be wrestling with in life and propose answers … well thought out theological solutions. It just might be worth trying!

"Faith, I think that I've finally figured out what I want to pursue in the coming weeks … writing short exposés to modern society's challenges."

Faith smiled to herself, her back to Barclay. She replied, "Great idea, dear. How did you come up with such a concept?"

After all, it was better for Barclay to take the credit for such an undertaking, than to remind him that it was she who planted the seeds to such an exercise. Love has many avenues of expression!

Chapter Two

BARCLAY hurriedly finished breakfast to retire to his study. After completing his private morning devotions, he settled before his Apple computer eager to begin an attempt to address a topic that he observed had been surfacing in this modern age for years ... the value of mandatory church attendance.

This is the one issue that had been so often put to him in one form or another during his rectorship at St. Bart's. He never felt it was appropriate to address the controversy in a sermon to his regular church attendees. After all, they were the faithful in weekly church attendance. "No use preaching to the choir," he had always reasoned.

It seemed that such questions were surfacing more frequently in the media ... especially in letters to the editor of newspapers and articles in journals widely read by non-church people.

They all seemed to follow a similar theme:

"I don't need to go to church to be religious!"

"I can worship God in my fishing boat, at the cottage, or on the golf course, just as well as sitting in a pew."

"I prefer to watch T.V. preachers on Sunday morning. They are much more entertaining."

But the one argument that was the most upsetting to Barclay was the blatant statement: "I don't get anything out of church! It is boring!"

Barclay had no idea how his response to their questions could be published, if indeed ever, but he knew that to address such statements would be personally therapeutic. With a fresh cup of coffee, double cream, next to his right hand, he relished the challenge to put words to paper. Words flowed with ease.

TO NON-ATTENDERS AT PUBLIC WORSHIP

We've all heard it said: "I don't go to church because I get nothing out of it. I can be just as religious as church goers through my own private devotions."

Well friends, I beg to differ!

Let me put it as bluntly as possible: One does not go to church to *get*. One goes to church to *give*. Going to worship is paying the incredible debt one owes to God. If one gets anything beyond doing so, well that accusation is a gift ... a bonus!

Let us focus on the two verbs "get" and "give."

Christ paid the supreme price for the sins of the world: His life on the cross for the salvation of humanity ... His blood shed as a sacrifice for our trespasses. Grace, it's called ... unmerited love for those who don't deserve it: The greatest demonstration of *giving* the world has witnessed, and ever will again. Dare we then not *give* God thanks for the sacrifice of His Son?

For without His sacrifice, not one of us will be able to stand in His presence. The Anglican Book of Common prayer makes it crystal clear: "We are not worthy so much as to gather the crumbs under Thy table."

In turn, Christians thus are obligated to give back to God. The Book of Common Prayer again lays it before us: " … here we offer and present unto thee, O Lord, ourselves, our souls and bodies, to be a reasonable, holy, and living sacrifice unto thee. And although we are unworthy, yet we beseech thee to accept this our bounden duty and service, not weighing our merits, but pardoning our offences …."

"Bounden duty and service" … try applying these concepts on a seat on a fishing boat, or on the eighteenth green of a golf course on a Sunday morning!

Christians do not go to worship to *get*. They go to *give* themselves, their souls and bodies, their talents, a percentage of their resources, their time, their thanks, and gratitude for what God in Christ has done for them.

For some, it is entirely possible that in so doing, one may indeed come away feeling they received nothing out of worship that morning. But that is a moot argument. If one attends worship to *get*, one has already missed the point. *Getting* is not the same as *giving*. True worship is not entertainment! True worship is the art of paying homage to God!

Historical Christianity has always maintained that "one can have a personal relationship with Christ, but not a private one." For Christians are the gathered body of Christ with many members. St Paul states: "We are members of one another" (Ephesians 4:25) and "To each is given the manifestation of the Spirit for the common good" (I Corinthians 12:7).

The fact is baptism and the Holy Eucharist cannot be self-administered. The laying on of hands and anointing with Holy Oil cannot be self-applied. What makes anyone think that private Christianity is valid? For to argue that such a private life in Christ is sufficient is to completely ignore the necessity of the partaking of the sacraments ... especially the Holy Eucharist.

For St. John's Gospel states: "Truly, truly, I say to you, unless you eat of the flesh of the Son of man and drink his blood, you have no life in you" (John 6:53).

Consequently, if one accepts these words of Jesus as His mandate for sacramental worship, then certainly one does *get* ... receives, from attending church. The very presence of Christ Himself in the bread and wine! To then argue that one takes away nothing by attending public worship is to entirely miss the point! Case dismissed!

Popular culture has conditioned this age to believe that unless an event is entertaining, pleasurable, a diversion from the status quo, it is to be avoided. With one's salvation at stake I argue: worship is serious business ... not an act of amusement or self-gratification.

Now, of course, my argument for mandatory public worship is based on a fundamental premise: that God exists.

If God exists, then there must be consequences for not acknowledging His divinity. It would be absurd to believe that the Creator does not expect one's submission to His dominion ... His sovereignty.

But, if God doesn't exist, then humanity is free to make up the rules for living ... rules that are changeable ... flexible ... not set in stone.

Consequently, each individual has to decide for oneself: "Yes" or "No" to God's existence.

Quite a gamble, is it not? Humanity can't prove that God exists, nor can humankind prove that God doesn't exist! It's the starting foundation to every decision a human being must face in life. Everything else depends on this fundamental first premise for one's existence: morals, ethics, behaviour, how one treats others, priorities, what and which personal "gods" one will bow down to.

So here's the question: Do you believe that God exists? If the answer is yes, then you have an obligation to worship Him. If the answer is no, and you are free to say that, then don't expect God, if He does exist, to say to you on Judgment Day, "Are you still bored?"

* * *

Barclay's first draft of his treatise was personally rewarding. He felt tired … drained of energy … but at the same time elated that he had penned a response to counter secular society's dismissal of the need of organized Christian worship. He had no idea what to do with his rough draft of rebuttal. "Maybe time will open doors for me to be published," he thought to himself.

"Barclay, time for lunch," Faith shouted down to his study.

"Faith, that was the shortest morning I've had in a long time. What is on the menu?"

"Leftovers from last night's dinner!"

"Leftovers! Leftovers! Faith, I just completed an article that I should have addressed years ago, but never found time to do so. I'm just worried that it may be a leftover … maybe never to be shared with anyone … never published. I'm not sure that I like leftovers!"

"You will today, dear! There's one last leftover piece of blueberry pie with your name on it."

Chapter Three

THE Steadmore's high-rise condo on the tenth floor overlooked the water in Trinity Harbour. It was the perfect location for retirement. No grass to cut … no snow to shovel … underground parking for their Mustang convertible. The two bedroom, fifteen-hundred square-foot unit was self-contained with an ensuite bath off the main bedroom, another bathroom for guests to use, and a laundry room off the main hallway. One small area in the master bedroom was used as a study where their Apple computer served the needs of both Faith and Barclay.

There was one area most frequented by both of them during the summer months and warm spring and fall days … a large balcony with an entrance from the den. The entire harbour below was a great view … the perfect area to watch the comings and goings of Trinity Harbour's Yacht Club members. After breakfast, the two retirees usually sat high above the water's edge, reading the town's morning newspaper and drinking coffee.

Life was good! Faith volunteered once a week at the town's Downtown Mission, helping to serve the evening meal to the usual crowd of approximately 130 hungry family members and the small group of people who could be identified as homeless.

Barclay, for the first few months of his retirement, was content to read and to research on the computer ... catching up on recent theological articles published by contemporary theologians.

It was almost a month ago that he had admitted to Faith that he was restless ... feeling ready to again put ink to paper. Faith had encouraged him to do just that ... knowing that her husband needed a challenge to keep his mind active, and begin a somewhat disciplined routine in his retirement. She was right, of course. As a result, Barclay wrote the first article which he entitled "To Non-Attenders at Public Worship."

It was so therapeutic for the old weekly crafter of sermons that Barclay was determined to keep writing on a somewhat scheduled basis ... three mornings a week ... Mondays, Tuesdays, and Thursdays. He was again feeling that in some way, even as a retired cleric, he might be fulfilling his call to ordained ministry.

How, he wasn't sure! In the meantime, he simply labelled the growing, completed, unpublished editorials, for lack of a better term, *The Steadmore Chronicles*.

"Bark, isn't this your morning for meeting with your fellow coffeeholics? It is now 9:30 a.m. and you three usually gather at 10:00 a.m.," Faith, breaking the silence, inquired of her husband as they sat in comfortable chairs on the balcony.

"You're right, Faith. I'll have a quick shower and shave and I think that I can make it in the nick of time," replied Barclay as he dashed to the bathroom.

It was Friday morning, the one day of the week when the three retired clerics in Trinity Harbour gathered at the Bean Bar, the busiest coffee shop in town.

A short time after the Steadmores had moved to town, Barclay, making his usual coffee run on a Friday morning, ran into the two clerics huddled in a booth in the busy coffee shop. Since both of them were wearing their clerical collars, Barclay introduced himself, was invited to join the two, and a warm friendship began. If one failed to show up on a Friday morning, a quick call was made to the absent comrade, inquiring why they were "stood up," as they jokingly put it.

Barclay made it with two minutes to spare.

Father David Antonopoulos, the retired Greek Orthodox priest, and Father Joseph Murphy, a retired Roman Catholic priest, rose to greet Barclay, shaking his hand and motioned him to join them. All three were not wearing their clericals, as usual. Anyone coming in for a quick coffee and dessert would not have known that the three were clerics.

"You were just about to get a call, Steadmore," teased Fr. Murphy. "Can't keep up the pace any longer now that you are retired? Having trouble with that Mustang of yours failing to start?"

"I don't drive a Russian LADA, Joe, but I can't afford a Lexus, like you drive. We Anglicans are frugal folks," came back Barclay. Fr. Murphy grinned and reminded his friend that he inherited the SUV when a rich uncle in Alberta died and willed him his favourite ride.

The three decided what they wanted to order and it was Barclay's turn to pay. He left the two in the booth, went to the order counter and purchased the morning treats.

Their morning conversation quickly turned to a discussion of the theological concerns of the secular age. It was obvious that denominational affiliations had little difference common to their own pastoral experiences.

The range of topics was broad:

declining numbers in the pews, the demanding task of fundraising for the needy, ever increasing repair costs for the upkeep of church buildings, secular events held on Sunday mornings drawing people away from worship, the popular seemingly acceptance of society to claim that all world religions are equal in the eye of God, and worst of all, New Age Religious gatherings ever increasing in membership.

The three clerics often needed a second cup of coffee to extend their stay together. Barclay increasingly was convinced that he was not alone when it came to his convictions. In a war with secular society it was great to find like-minded clerics sharing his concerns, especially coming from such denominations as the Orthodox and Roman Catholic faiths.

Friday by Friday, it became obvious that the three were on the same page theologically. After each morning gathering, Barclay went home and jotted down the topics discussed. He wasn't sure why he took such careful notes, but he was soon to discover why.

Chapter Four

"**BARK,** it's for you!" Faith handed the portable phone over to her husband who was reading the morning edition of the *Trinity Harbour Post*.

"Who is it Faith?"

"Didn't recognize the number that came up. The caller asked for the Canon Doctor Steadmore."

"Good morning! This is Barclay Steadmore."

"Good morning Dr. Steadmore. My name is James Parker. I'm the editor of the *Tangleville Mirror*. Am I calling at a time convenient for you?"

"Yes, I'm just finishing today's morning newspaper. Can I help you?"

It is interesting how clergy never get away from active ministry … even following retirement. "Can I help you?" was the way Barclay had often answered the office phone when he was the former rector of St. Bartholomew's parish in Tangleville. Old habits do die slowly.

"Doctor, I have a proposition which I'd like to discuss with you in person. It will take some time to outline. Is there any possibility that you might meet with me in my office, say within the coming five days?"

"Mr. Parker, my spouse and I are going to be in Tangleville this coming Wednesday. We've been invited by Harry Sting to be present for his swearing-in ceremony on town council that evening. Would a meeting in the morning of Wednesday work for you?"

"How about 10:00 a.m.? I will set aside an hour for us to discuss a proposal I'd like to offer to you."

"Yes, I can make it! Will you give me a hint as to what you wish to discuss?"

"I'd rather lay it out with you in person. I think you may be interested after you hear what I've been working on. OK?"

"Fair enough! See you this coming Wednesday. Goodbye."

Barclay leaned back in his large leather reclining chair, his feet on the footstool before him … the newspaper on the floor to his right.

"Well, that was a strange call Faith. It was James Parker, the editor of the *Tangleville Mirror*. I've been invited to meet with him this coming Wednesday, at 10:00 a.m. He wouldn't give me any information about why. What do you think he's up to?"

Over their many years of marriage, Faith had demonstrated time and time again an uncanny ability to predict future events. In their early days of marriage, it troubled Barclay, ever the rational one. But Faith was so intuitive, clued into an awareness of things without conscious reasoning that he came to accept that it was a gift that he would never understand … nor want to.

"I'll bet that it has something to do with a position to fill in his newspaper. Maybe he needs a columnist of some kind … someone to shake up his readership. Would you be prepared to do that?"

"Oh Faith, it can't be! I'm too far out of Tangleville to do something like that … maybe even too old to tackle such an undertaking.

Besides, since we moved from Tangleville some time ago, nobody may even remember me now. You've got to be mistaken!"

Faith smiled and gave him a peck on the cheek. "We'll see," she said. "If I am wrong, I'll take you out for dinner after church on Sunday. But if I'm right, what do you owe me?"

"I'm not going there," replied Barclay. Besides, he knew better than to question Faith's intuitive powers.

* * *

Barclay and Faith were to arrive on the Tuesday afternoon before Harry's big day. Harry and Annie were expecting them as guests for a few nights. The arrangements had been made shortly after Harry called to announce that he had been successful in winning a seat on council.

"Should we call ahead and tell Harry that I have an appointment with Parker, or simply inform him after we arrive?"

"No! Somehow I think Harry may know more about that call this morning than we may think. Let's wait and see how he responds to your announcement when we get there."

It was an enjoyable trip back to Tangleville for they hadn't visited their former hometown in the last four months. Barclay and Faith stopped for coffee halfway on the route to Tangleville. It was such fun driving his Mustang convertible. He wanted to put the top down, but Faith insisted that he not do so … "It messes up my hair," she said. "I don't want to look a mess when we arrive at the Stings."

The couple pulled into the Sting driveway at precisely 3:15 p.m. Harry was not home, but Annie was waiting for them … coffee and shortbread cookies waiting. It was a warm greeting!

Barclay carried their luggage to the Stings' spare bedroom and the three settled into the den ... drinking coffee, snacking, and getting caught up on how the two families were making out since the Steadmores had moved away to Trinity Harbour.

"Harry will be home around 5:30 p.m., Doctor," Annie said to Barclay. "Why don't you take an afternoon nap while Faith and I continue with our conversation? I'll call you when Harry arrives. Dinner will be served about 7:00 p.m."

Barclay needed no further urging to take Annie's suggestion. Since retirement, he always enjoyed a short rest period in the afternoon.

"Call me when Harry arrives, Annie. I can't wait to see him again."

* * *

Faith gave a gentle knock on the bedroom door, roused Barclay from a sound sleep, and announced, "Harry's home. He wants to see you!"

The two old friends warmly embraced and settled down into the den ... quizzing each other about what the other had been doing over the past few months. Their conversation was spirited and enthusiastic.

Harry informed Barclay that after winning a seat on council, he'd resigned from his radio show host position at AM KNOW. "It was not an easy decision, Barclay ... a bittersweet move. But it had to be done! I don't want other members of council saying that I have a bully pulpit in the town. It is going to be tough enough that many over the years already have formed opinions as to how I may vote on contentious issues coming before council. I want to be recognized as a man of conviction ... someone who is consistent with one's Biblical principles. After all, I was elected by Christians to do no other."

"Harry, I know you! You can do it if anyone can. The one thing you are going to have to look out for is 'political correctness.' Political correctness will bite you every time. If you ever get into a situation where conscience and political expediency collide, call me! I'm on your side. You know that."

Barclay didn't get around to telling Harry about his call from the editor of the *Tangleville Mirror* before Annie announced that dinner was served. Harry had so many topics to bring up to Barclay that the time between his friend's nap and the beginning of their time in the den, that Harry said, "Let's continue after we eat. I want to hear about how you have been putting in your retirement days."

Harry said the grace before the meal, and the four took an hour and a half to enjoy a fabulous meal of roast beef, Yorkshire pudding, turnip and squash, mashed potatoes, and dark brown gravy ... finishing with homemade rice pudding and apple pie. Barclay tried a little of both. Coffee and tea completed the meal.

"Harry and Annie, I have to beg off for a couple of hours tomorrow morning. I have an appointment with James Parker over at the office of the *Tangleville Mirror*. I have no idea what is up, but I promised him that I'd listen to something he wants to discuss with me. Any idea Harry what it is all about?"

There was a brief moment of silence before Harry grinned that coy smile of his ... a smile that hinted that he was already in on the meeting.

"Can't speak to the matter, Barclay!"

Political correctness was already in its developmental stage in Harry's life! For the word "can't" has a number of meanings!

Barclay was about to push Harry for a clear answer when he felt a slight kick on the shin under the table. Faith was giving him that "no" look. Barclay quickly moved to another topic.

Chapter Five

FOLLOWING a light breakfast on Wednesday morning, the four discussed their plans for the day. Annie and Faith were going shopping at the Tangleville Mall. Harry had a 9:30 a.m. appointment at the Town Hall ... a rehearsal for the evening swearing-in ceremony and following the rehearsal, a seminar to acquaint council members for the next series of weekly council meetings.

Harry had been supplied with reams of documentation shortly after the announcement of his new seat on council. He had meticulously read and reread the material in preparation for the day's seminar. There were still many questions to be answered. He was looking forward to the day's workshop.

Barclay was excited! What was James Parker at the *Tangleville Mirror* going to propose? He had been intrigued by what Faith had predicted might transpire... an offer of some sort of a columnist or guest editorial writer.

"No", he thought as he drove his Mustang to the parking lot of the downtown newspaper edifice, "I'm not sure even if Faith's prediction is accurate, that I'd even be interested. Besides, why would Parker want me? There are plenty of qualified spillers of ink already in Tangleville. Nah, it can't be so."

Barclay was ten minutes early for the appointment. After he introduced himself to the receptionist in the foyer of the rather impressive building, he took a seat in a big comfortable padded chair and waited for his host to appear.

Instead, a smartly dressed woman approached him and introduced herself. "I am Samantha Birkley, Mr. Parker's assistant editor. We've been looking forward to our time with you. Follow me, please, to Mr. Parker's office."

"Didn't expect to be interviewed by two people," Barclay thought to himself. "They must be serious about something."

Samantha led Barclay into Mr. Parker's office, a large room with big black leather chairs around a coffee table and a long conference table surrounded by twelve chairs. Mr. Parker's desk was located on the opposite side of the room from the seating area. Mr. Parker, a man who appeared to be in his late forties, immaculately attired in a dark gray business suit and a conservative blue tie, promptly rose to meet them.

"Doctor Steadmore, this is James Parker. Mr. Parker … Doctor Steadmore."

James quickly approached Barclay, firmly extended an outstretched hand, and directed his guest to a seat at the conference table. James sat in the chair at the end of the table, obviously the location he used during board meetings, and Samantha sat across from Barclay, the two of them on either side of Mr. Parker, within arm's reach of each other.

"Thank-you for coming, Doctor," James began. "We've been looking forward to meeting with you. We have plans that we hope will involve your participation. Let me lay them out before you!"

It was obvious to Barclay that Mr. Parker was a man used to wielding power. He wasn't wasting time in coming to the point of the meeting.

"For some time during the past months, before and during the lead up to the formation of the now established Tangleville Christian Coalition, a prominent member of the town's clergy, The Reverend Doctor Angus McLaughlin, wrote a weekly column for our newspaper. It was so well read that it resulted in a larger than expected number of letters to the editor following each of his articles ... both pro and con in nature. Doctor McLaughlin has retired and we are searching for a replacement for him ... someone who will carry on the tradition that he began. We think that you may be just the cleric to do so!"

"So that is what it's all about," Barclay thought to himself. "It's about business, controversy, and contention: Faith was not far off in her prediction of why I was contacted."

The memories of how he and Harry used to spar on the radio show years ago resurfaced. Was he really interested in once again assuming such a role in Tangleville? It was, after all, a time of fun and intellectual gymnastics.

"Well, I'm here," thought Barclay. "Why not pursue the matter and see if I can possibly turn such an offer into a positive one for the Christian community? I've nothing to lose if I push for editorial freedom. I can simply say that I'm not the person for the position. Let's see how much latitude I can wring out of these two people if I agree to be interested by their offer."

"Well, Mr. Parker and Ms. Birkely, I'm somewhat surprised by your request." Barclay wasn't about to admit to them about Faith's prediction. "There are many details that we would have to pursue for me to agree to such an undertaking. Shall we discuss them?"

"Of course, Doctor, but first let us outline a job description of what we have in mind. Samantha, will you do that for us?"

Samantha handed around a one page document detailing the requirements for the position. They included:

- A weekly column to appear in each Friday edition of the *Tangleville Mirror*;
- Topics to be addressed are to be controversial in nature;
- Political correctness must be adhered to in all articles;
- Articles submitted became the sole property of the newspaper;
- The editor(s) have the right to reject and/or edit all submissions before publication;
- The Newspaper will state that all published submissions are not necessarily the view of the *Tangleville Mirror*;
- The Newspaper will not defend the columnist of published articles in the possibility of a lawsuit for opinions stated in all submissions;
- A monetary penalty will be assessed in case the columnist fails to submit a weekly article on time for publication;
- An honorarium will be paid to the columnist at the end of each month (amount to be mutually agreed upon);
- The contract will be for a one-year term with the option of the columnist or the Newspaper to extend or cancel the position by giving two weeks' notice.

Doctor Steadmore took a full five minutes to read the job description and requirements for articles submitted. When he finished perusing the document, he placed it before him on the table, turned it face down, and sat in silence. He made every effort not to display a facial gesture of approval or disapproval of what he had just read.

James Parker broke the silence. "Well Doctor, what do you think of our offer?"

"I think that you have the wrong person before you today. Thank-you so much for considering me as the one to replace Doctor McLaughlin. Good luck in finding such a columnist!"

Barclay feigned an effort to arise from the table to leave.

Before Barclay was able to stand, James rose to his feet and motioned Barclay to return to his chair.

"Doctor Steadmore, we are most serious in having you join our editorial staff. The job description we presented to you is a standard one that is required of all our employees who submit articles for publication. Obviously they don't meet with your approval or standards. Can't we at least hear the concerns which so clearly motivated you to not pursue our offer?"

Barclay sat down again in his chair, knowing that the two before him were likely to make concessions to acquire his services.

"Mr. Parker, and Ms. Birkley, you must realize that I am a cleric … a priest in the Christian church. In my entire ministry … sermons and articles published … personal relationships with groups and individuals, I never … repeat never … spoke, wrote, or addressed others in a fashion that I didn't think was anything but truthful, honest, and reflective of the Holy Scriptures. I'm not about to begin now! If I were to consider your offer, I would never write an article that I didn't believe precisely coincided with my Christian views. I admit not all readers would agree with views that offend them. But I will not write to deliberately turn people against me or the orthodox standards of the Christian church.

"I'll admit that what I've just said is a bit of a sermon. I didn't mean for it to be so, but you must understand what is non-negotiable."

Mr. Parker glanced over at Ms. Birkley, and back to Barclay. "Is there more we need to hear about?"

"Yes, indeed. I cannot accept the clause that my editorial submissions would be subject to alterations by your editorial staff, nor that I would have to adhere to political correctness. Political correctness is a sense of censorship in itself ... a form of power control that many are beginning to question. If our Lord was to be writing and speaking in our modern age, He would be censored by those who might wish to silence Him. Of course, some forms of political correctness make sense, but the writer must be free to choose one's words to accurately convey the message."

"We're listening, Doctor. Is there more you would like us to hear?"

"Yes, but not so objectionable, that I don't think that they could be rectified. Of course, your newspaper must state with each of my articles, if I agree to write them, a statement something like the following:

'The opinions expressed in this editorial are not necessarily the views of the *Tangleville Mirror*.' That's perfectly fair.

"And there is another matter I need to bring forward. I would not be willing to write a weekly column. After all, I'm retired. I would be willing, however, to consider a column to be submitted twice a month ... with time off accordingly for my spouse and I to take a vacation. And, most importantly, I would insist that I have the freedom to name the title for the article … just as Dr. McLaughlin did when he used the heading 'The Cleric Speaks.'"

"Is there anything else Dr. Steadmore?"

"No! That just about outlines my objections to your offer."

Mr. Parker rose from his chair, shook Barclay's hand, and replied,

"Would you mind stepping out of my office for a few minutes? Samantha and I need to talk. There is coffee available in the reception area. Don't go away. We will call you in a few minutes!"

Barclay didn't reply to James's request, but readily exited the room. The two couldn't see the expression on his face, but he was smiling.

It seemed like a rather long few minutes before James Parker appeared in the reception area and greeted Barclay with the following words:

"Doctor, will you please join Samantha and me? We want you to hear us out. We think that we have an offer that you can't refuse!"

Barclay followed James back to his office and took his former seat.

James began.

"Doctor Steadmore, thank-you for being straightforward and honest with us today. As a priest, we know that you would not do otherwise. We want you also to know that as a priest, you must tell it as you understand your Christian convictions. Doctor McLaughlin did exactly that in his articles and we trust that you would do no other. Here's what we are prepared to offer you.

"Complete editorial freedom, unrestricted choice of topics, no editing of your submissions, and no insistence on political correctness, trusting in you to do so as you deem it fair and just. A twice-monthly submission will be fine. We would prefer a weekly one, but we can live with your request."

James paused to give Barclay an opportunity to respond.

Barclay in a measured fashion replied: "So far, I like what I am hearing."

"We can work around your concern about time off with plenty of advance notice on your behalf. Now we must, however, discuss your honorarium. What did you have in mind?"

Barclay had given this question no advanced thought. He wasn't really concerned about the financial side of the position, but without hesitation, he replied:

"I'll leave that up to your discretion. However, whatever is deemed fair, make the monthly cheque out to The Samaritan Inn here in Tangleville. I do hope that you will be somewhat generous, as that organization is doing great work! Oh, and one more thing … I will submit a mileage request to you whenever I come and go from my residence for meetings with you here in town. Fair enough?"

James and Samantha rose from their chairs, extending hands to shake Barclay's. "Do we have a deal then Dr. Steadmore?" asked James.

"A deal!" grinned Barclay, as he closed the offer with a firm handshake with both of them. "Oh, by the way, who submitted my name to your newspaper, anyway?"

"Harry Sting!"

Faith was right again!

Chapter Six

AS Barclay drove back to the Sting residence, his mind was reeling. What was he getting himself into? Would Faith be in agreement with this new chapter in his life? What was he going to submit as his first article to the *Tangleville Mirror*?

This last concern, he suddenly realized, was the easiest to answer. He had already written an article on mandatory Sunday worship. Why not submit that for publication? It might take a little polishing, but that would be easy to do. When he wrote it, he had no idea where or when it might be made public. Now a door had opened. Such a door at the time could never have been thought to exist. God surely does work in mysterious ways!

* * *

The swearing-in ceremony at the Tangleville Town Hall for incoming town councillors, the nine former returning re-elected members and the three new first timers, Harry and two women, was an impressive event. The ceremony was brief, about twenty minutes in length. The proceedings began with a politically correct theological invocation, a prayer designed to affront no one, delivered by the recording secretary of Town Council ... read from a collection of set approved prayers. No one was offended and no one recognized any Christian content whatsoever.

"OK," thought Harry. "Such are the times in our secular society!"

Following the formal ceremony of the swearing-in process, an elaborate reception took place. It was a time to mingle ... press the flesh, so to speak, and be interviewed and photographed by the local media. With Annie by his side, both smartly attired, they made an impressive couple.

Harry was singularly cornered by those in attendance, wishing to introduce them to him and take selfies. He, of course, was so well known because of being the host of his long time former radio show. Many in the town knew only his voice, but not his appearance. A number of people asked Harry if he was going to shake up the proceedings on council.

Harry would only reply, "I'll do my best to represent the good people of Ward One here in town." He was well on his way to giving a politically correct answer.

On the way home, all four—Harry, Annie, Faith, and Barclay, in Harry's Audi—evaluated the event. Harry was especially elated! There were so many people who had lined up to meet him and who had wished him well.

"But what do you think that means?" Harry quizzed his riders. "What did they mean when they used the expression 'wish me well'? Were those code words to warn me of conflict ahead on council? ... That I have work to do as a Christian councillor? Were they suggesting that I am expected to infuse my Christian faith into council voting? Am I as a Christian, who has not hidden my faith, expected to be in opposition to the status quo?" Harry's questions came fast and furious. It was obvious that being elected was now becoming a reality in his life.

The three riders let Harry get his thoughts out into the open. With few interjections, they tried to reassure him of the fact that he would be up to the task.

"Harry, let's take it one day at a time. You have no idea what lies before you in upcoming council meetings. So don't let hypothetical problems concern you. Enjoy the day! Celebrate it!" replied Annie.

"Harry, you are not alone in this," reassured Barclay. "God has brought you to this point in your life for a purpose. Remember the words of the Anglican Book of Alternative Services Prayer Book:

'Glory to God,

Whose power working in us can do

infinitely more than we can ask or imagine.'

"You've said it countless times at the end of the liturgy. Now is the time to believe those words belong especially to you."

They were only a few blocks from the Sting residence when Barclay thought that it might be the time to change the subject and inform the three others of his morning meeting at the *Tangleville Mirror*.

By the time that they pulled into the driveway, Barclay had

outlined his new position at the Newspaper and was delighted that Faith, on learning of his acceptance, was firmly in support of his decision.

"You need a new challenge, Bark! I'm all for it. Now you will not find time on your hands following your retirement." She didn't say it, but she was certain that the time required to write the twice monthly submissions would free her from making suggestions as to how he could put his many talents into productive research ... to keep him at times out of her hair!

Annie seemed to be surprised by Barclay's news. Harry was unusually silent in asking details of Barclay's new position.

"Harry, thank-you for setting it all up! I know that you were working behind the scenes. You already are learning the art of pulling strings, just as a successful politician should do," teased Barclay.

Harry smiled and answered, "No comment!" ... words that he may have to use many times in the future as a town councillor.

"He'll do just fine," Barclay thought to himself. "I just hope that he can walk the line between his Christian convictions and the demands of the secular culture."

Chapter Seven

THEY were a busy two weeks for Barclay following the interview with James Parker and Samantha Birkley in the Tangleville Mirror office. The major terms of the agreement had been finalized with their handshakes, but it was left up to Samantha and Barclay to cross the "T's" and dot the "I's" in the final details of the contract.

A number of e-mails flowed back and forth. It was agreed that before any of Barclay's submissions were to be published that the newspaper would prepare the readership for the advent of his columns.

The task was completed when Samantha e-mailed Barclay the prepared editorial to be published the week before Barclay's first publication.

> ANNOUNCEMENT
>
> In the coming weeks, a new twice-monthly column will appear in this newspaper. We, as editors, think that you will become avid readers of this new addition which is likely to be thought provoking and even entertaining. You may find yourself in agreement with or possibly irritated by what you read. Either way, we

feel that you will become loyal followers of our newly-acquired team member of the *Tangleville Mirror*. The column will be entitled:

THE TANGLEVILLE CHRONICLES

Does Father Know Best?

It will be submitted by the Rev. Canon Dr. Barclay Steadmore, the former rector of St. Bartholomew's Anglican Parish here in town, now retired and living in Trinity Harbour. Dr. Steadmore has been granted full editorial licence to choose the topics and contents to be published, without our newspaper altering in anyway what he submits to us. We, of course, will end every submission by Dr. Steadmore with the disclaimer:

"The contents of this article are solely the views of the writer and no way are affirmed or denied by this newspaper."

You, as readers, are strongly encouraged to submit letters to the editor in either support or condemnation of Dr. Steadmore's articles. The best of these letters may be published by us and forwarded to Dr. Steadmore. You, of course, must be willing to sign your letter with your name and general home location. Submissions will not be returned to the senders.

Samantha Birkley, Assistant Editor

Barclay forwarded a polished version of that article he had written weeks ago entitled "To Non-Attenders at Public Worship" as his first submission. The aftermath was just as expected. The readership was divided with almost half in full agreement of his views, while those upset were zealously opposed to his condemnation of private religion. The editors of the newspaper were delighted, as all publishers cherish controversy! Dissension ... arguments sell newspapers!

Barclay, upon receiving e-mails of the letters to the editor, read them with satisfaction, knowing that his first submission was touching people's lives. Religion, it seemed, was still very much alive in the secular world. Some want to further the role of the sacred, while others hope to eliminate all forms of religious demands to the annals of history. Barclay knew that he was on the right track. Future articles must arouse a complacent culture.

* * *

This new role as columnist was certainly going to demand more of Barclay's time in front of his Mac. Two weeks between articles seemed to be a reasonable length of time to prepare his two submissions per month to the *Tangleville Mirror*, but Barclay was not the type of person to leave such a matter to the last moment. What he really wanted to do was to have a number of submissions ready, far in advance of each two week period ... a bank of completed articles ready in case he and Faith may wish to take some time off together ... a short vacation ... a hedge against unforeseen illness that might prevent him from composing.

Since his first article was obviously a success, he put aside a number of already completed essays, filed them as possible future submissions ... and decided to write his second column designed to complement in some way his first.

A statement which he had heard and intrigued him for a number of years before seemed to be one to investigate. It would become his second submission.

IT IS NOT YOUR FAULT, BUT IT IS YOUR PROBLEM
Does Father Know Best?
by The Rev. Canon Dr. Barclay Steadmore

Let me preface this column with the words of the Serenity Prayer written by the American Theologian, Reinhold Niebuhr (1892-1971). The short version reads: "God grant me the serenity to accept the things I cannot change, courage to change the things I can, and wisdom to know the difference."

We live in a culture that is increasingly becoming convinced that individuals are being held hostage to the ever-increasing consequences of modern living … where more and more people are experiencing zero control over their lives … where the past seems to be deemed as irrelevant. Hence, the expression: "It's not my fault, but it is my problem." And it certainly is a "my" problem: yours and mine.

It is not one's fault if while driving in a responsible, careful manner, a drunk driver runs a red light and one ends up in the emergency ward.

It is not one's fault if one loses one's source of employment when a company decides to move to another city or country where labour costs are cheaper.

It is not your fault if your home is broken into and valuables are stolen … and an escape clause in the insurance policy deems your claim to be null and void.

It is not your fault when a company decides that your job is no longer needed because a robot can do the task more accurately.

There are so many ways that individuals are being relegated to "zero" control of their lives … but it is their problem!

Admit it! There are areas of life one can definitely not control! In such cases, Richard Niebuhr's Serenity Prayer applies … perhaps the only solution to such cases that is effective, because Niebuhr began the prayer with a call to God. God's intervention! When nothing else in the world can be relied upon for healing. Peace in the midst of chaos. Trust that God is ultimately in control. As the modern saying goes: "Get over it" ... Move on! Trust God!

There are situations in life in which one may say, "It's not my fault" when indeed it "is my problem," and it is able to be solved. It is called accountability! It is taking ownership of the status quo ... saying "I didn't contribute to the problem, but I can contribute to the solution."

For Christians, this last statement is one that is applicable to all life's problems, but particularly to secular society's Goliath attempts to abrogate religion to the archives of morality and influence in the public square.

There is an old bluegrass song with the lyrics stating: "I'm not broke, but I'm badly bent."

Many Christians feel this way in today's age. Christian values were once accepted as the standard for society's morals, conduct, and ethical practices ... thought to be society's conscience, the foundation for upright and proper behaviour in society. But Christians, for some time now, are feeling rejected and advised to keep one's faith standards private. "Think it, but don't say it!"

Christians greeted others universally with the expression "Merry Christmas." Now it is "Happy Holidays." There is no recognition of Christ in the latter phrase.

"A blessed Easter" once was the common greeting. Now Easter is the celebration of bunnies and coloured eggs ... the ownership of the commercial world. Do we dare say "God bless you" when a person sneezes? We may but offend an atheist in so doing.

The public school system is now by law free from Christian religious celebrations, as well as those of all the great world religions. In our modern society, in which there is separation between religion and the state, this can be reluctantly tolerated by Christians, never-the-less, remembering the past when the educational system was expected to reinforce the values of the church and home settings. In a multicultural society, such is the law, and Christians respect the laws of the land. Christians do not believe in exerting control over things they cannot control.

However, Christians are free to focus efforts on that which is still open to them ... areas of society where secularism still has not consumed human conduct.

The Fundamental Freedoms section of the Canadian Charter of Rights and Freedoms states (paraphrased and commentary):

"Everyone has the following fundamental freedoms:

(a) freedom of conscience and religion;

(b) freedom of thought, belief, opinion, and expression, including freedom of the press and other media of communication;

(c) freedom of peaceful assembly; and

(d) freedom of association."

Who then can prevent Christians from saying "Merry Christmas" instead of "Happy Holidays?" No one!

Who can prevent individual Christians from speaking everyday conversations with others with such use of words as "my parish," "my priest," or "my minister?" No One!

We are free to wear Christian symbols, which without words convey to others that we are members of the Body of Christ. We are free to display Christian settings for Christmas and Easter on our own front lawns, and free to attach Christian symbols on our vehicles. Christians need to remain focused on what is possible today and tomorrow.

In the Book of Isaiah 40:3, the prophet states: "In the wilderness prepare the way of the Lord, make straight in the desert a highway for our God." The prophet's words are just as prophetic in modern times as they were before the time of Christ: poverty, addictions, injustice, racism, disease, educational inequalities. Everyone has the power to say "yes" or "no" to demands made upon us. Niebuhr had it right! There are things that Christians can change. There are those we can't!

Grant us O Lord, the serenity to know the difference, and the courage and will to be agents of change in the kingdom when Christ gives us the opportunity to do so!

drsteadmore@starmail.com

Barclay pressed the "send" key. "I wonder what kind of response this submission will get?" he thought to himself. He was about to find out!

Chapter Eight

BARCLAY was on a roll. No sooner had he submitted his second article to the *Tangleville Mirror* that he felt compelled to begin to work on the next, even though it would not have to be ready for two weeks.

For years, he had wrestled with those two words: "political correctness." The secular insistence on this mentality irritated him to no small degree. Should a cleric, indeed any Christian, be constrained by this twentieth-century invention? How does "political correctness" stack up with the Holy Scriptures? Would Jesus, if He were here in the flesh in this century, adhere to modern society's demands in the retelling of the parables? Would He address issues of conduct between the sexes? Would He temper His words to satisfy those who might disagree with Him, the modern language police?

"If I am grappling with this concept, an invention of this age, surely others are as well," thought Barclay. "Why not take the issue head on? It may be a risky endeavour, but I'm going to confront the Leviathan face to face."

Sitting before his Mac, the words began to flow for his next submission.

IS IT BAD OR GOOD?

Does Father Know Best?

by The Rev. Canon Dr. Barclay Steadmore

What is another name for the expression, "Think it, but don't say it?"

If you answered: political correctness, you would be correct. Does the secular obligation to fall in line sit well with you? Do you agree with modern society's attempt to control your vocabulary? Is political correctness an attempt at censorship? Some will admit that we conform, but we don't believe in it. Is this then not hypocrisy?

In our modern age, it must be admitted that indeed certain aspects of political correctness are justified, even necessary. Christians ought to be the first to agree to this concept. Language that puts down, condemns, belittles, insults, is judgmental, is hateful, divides, or disadvantages individuals and groups is never the message of the Gospels. Love of neighbour and love of God out-rightly forbids such attitudes and vocabulary usage.

But this has not always been the case. Minorities in our societies have and still do experience disadvantages... Each of these groups has, and still does, experience disadvantages that the majority does not. Females have long understood and protested against the cultural acceptance of being considered second-class citizens. The Civil Rights Movement and the Women's Movements were far too long in coming to the forefront. All of the aforementioned groups are part of humanity, and they must be heard and understood as legitimate voices, not to be silenced nor put down by language that demeans and dismisses their articulate demands for justice.

Consequently, there is certainly the need to use non-sexist language when older versions of expression are now judged as out-of-date. There is no need to use the word "mankind" when the word "humankind" is more inclusive. Why would we not avoid offensive terms if we don't intend to offend anyone…

But have the modern thought police gone too far? I maintain such is the case and I refuse to go there!

Are you prepared to call homeless people "outdoor urban dwellers"? Dishonest people "ethically disoriented"? An insult, "emotional rape"? A right-wing protest a "riot," but a left-wing riot a "protest"? How about using the term "domestic engineer" to describe a housewife, or an "unplanned re-examination of recent food choices" instead of vomiting?

I believe that any reasonable and thoughtful individual gets the point. There is a limit to which the culture can be manipulated and bullied. As always, political correctness trumps common sense.

Whatever happened to the old expression "telling it like it is?" I believe society still admires an individual who is upfront and honest in stating what one believes and uses language that does not need to be second guessed.

If one has read the novel *1984* by George Orwell, who imagined a future world where speech was greatly restricted and censored, one may conclude that we are now living in Orwell's universe.

I end this article by stating that Christians need to be particularly on guard against secular society's attempts to sanitize history and to rewrite the Holy Scriptures, to translate them to use inclusive language. I, for one, refuse to transpose the expression "Father, Son, and Holy Spirit" to "Creator, Redeemer, and Sustainer." I know what lies behind the latter term … an attempt to neuter the former expression. The original manuscripts of the Old Testament and the New Testament are historical records, written in a fashion true to their age. Who are we to tamper with them?

God calls Christians to be authentic. A "Christmas tree" is not a "holiday tree" nor "Easter eggs" "Spring Spheres"!

God help us!

drsteadmore@starmail.com

Barclay pressed the "send" key and the second submission to "The Tangleville Chronicles" was on its way.

Chapter Nine

AS always, Barclay looked forward to his 10:00 a.m. Friday morning coffee with his two valued friends, fellow retired clerics Father David and Father Joseph. Barclay wanted to be there a little early to avoid being the last to show up because if he were a few minutes late again, Fr. Joseph would tease him about getting old and unable to keep up the pace now that he was retired.

Fr. Joseph was a walking encyclopaedia, a prodigious reader, very active in public affairs in Trinity Harbour, and one who kept up with current events in the world. A "go-to" guy if one needed advice on contentious theological issues in the twenty-first century.

Fr. David, the Greek Orthodox priest, was just the opposite of Fr. Joseph in so many ways. He exuded complete serenity in the midst of challenges in the contemporary changing world..

Unshaken in his faith and certain of the role of the church facing secularism's criticism in its "progressive" agents, he always maintained confidence in God's sovereignty. "We are not alone. God is in control. Be faithful and walk the walk," he was fond of saying.

Barclay was anxious to put his two brothers in Christ to work this morning. He had been wrestling with ideas for his next submission to the *Tangleville Mirror* without quite feeling secure in putting thoughts to paper. "I'm going to bend their minds this morning," he thought to himself as he fought the light traffic to the Bean Bar coffee shop. Pulling into the parking lot he was delighted that Fr. Joseph's Lexus SUV was not yet there. Fr. David's Ford Edge was just pulling in, and after the two exited, they walked side-by-side to find a seat for the three of them.

"Let's wait for Joseph," smiled David, as they chose a place off in the corner. "When he arrives, we'll tell him that it's his turn to buy since he has appeared to have forgotten our meeting. He'll object of course, but let's see if he'll buy it."

As luck would have it, Fr. Joseph arrived seven minutes late. When he came to greet his two friends, they both were extending the wrist watch exposed on their left arms and accusing him of being tardy.

Fr. Joseph was way ahead of them. Before they could insist on him buying the morning coffee, Fr. Joseph spoiled their little scam. "I'm buying today Fathers, but you are going to have to work for it. What will you have this morning?"

The two gave Fr. Joseph their orders, he approached the cashier, and he returned with their coffee and a large box of apple critters.

"Something's up," quipped Fr. David. "It looks like he's really preparing us for a lengthy session this morning."

Fr. Joseph smiled that sly smile of his and replied: "You are being tested! I need your advice on a potentially troublesome theological problem. Remember now, you are clerics. Ready?

"Just before Christmas I received a rather expensive Christmas card … not one of those purchased at a dollar store. Inside was a gift … a lottery ticket with instructions that the draw date would be three weeks after Christmas. The card was signed with the following greeting: 'In appreciation for what you did for me during a difficult time in my life. Merry Christmas!'

"Well, Fathers, there was no return address on the envelope. I've no idea as to the identity of the sender. I pinned the ticket to the bulletin board in my office and forgot about it. It is now four months after the draw date, and yesterday curiosity got the better of me. I took the ticket to the local convenience store and checked it out. To my astonishment, that ticket was the sole winner of a $2,000,000 draw. I'm now lost for a follow up. What should I do about what some folks would call my lucky day?"

"So does this mean that you are going to trade in your Lexus for a top of the line Porsche?" grinned Barclay.

"Come on now, Barclay. I'm already taking heat for driving my present SUV. I get teased that a priest must be one of those rich folk who have a healthy investment portfolio. I've already explained to you that it was an inheritance in an estate settlement. Otherwise there is no way I could afford it."

"So what's the problem, Joseph?" Fr. David wanted to know. "It is obvious that there is more behind your question than you have conveyed to us."

Fr. Joseph's smile turned to one of concern. "That's why I'm laying it out before the two of you today. Have another critter and tell me what I should do. What are my options as a priest? No, as a Christian, who has never purchased a lottery ticket in my entire life. I don't support state lotteries."

"Well, let's just list off a few considerations for you," came back Barclay. "And David, help me out.

"You can cash it in and put the money in the bank. You can't call it gambling, because you didn't buy the ticket in the first place. Technically, you are not guilty of being an accessory to a game of chance."

"Thought about that Barclay! But I can't seem to justify such a move. It is still unearned money. I feel that somehow God is testing me to live up to my convictions as a priest and as a Christian. No, there must be another solution."

"Another option, Joseph, is simply not to cash in the ticket. Problem solved!"

"No, that is not a solution, Barclay. I'm certain that the person or persons who sent me the anonymous card recorded the number on the ticket before sending it to me. If I don't cash it, the sender will think that I simply didn't appreciate the thoughtfulness and generosity behind the gift. A gift spurned, so to speak. And that is not my feelings at all. I know that whoever sent it did it out of love for me. I can't just not cash it!"

"If you don't cash it Joseph, the money will simply be upping the amount on the next lottery. Somebody, the next winner, will be happy that you didn't cash in. Remember, the computer system already knows that a winner is eligible for the prize. So don't think that by not claiming the prize, the lottery business will be somehow curtailed. All that will happen is, because of the next enhanced amount in the draw, more people will be encouraged to buy more tickets. The industry wins if you don't cash in. Do you want that to be the case?"

Fr. David had up to this point been silent. Ever the thoughtful, serene individual, he looked straight at Joseph and offered his advice.

"Joseph, have you considered that maybe God, in His infinite ways, has plans for that money, through you, to advance the Kingdom of Heaven?"

"Go on David, I'm listening."

"You must claim the money for a couple of reasons. It will give you a public pulpit like you may never have in the future. Claim the money. Have your picture taken holding the cheque. Wear your clerical collar and smile for the camera. When the reporters and the gaming company proudly shake your hand congratulating you, they will undoubtedly ask you what you are going to do with the windfall. Then you will have the opportunity to preach a sermon that will shock the secular crowd. Tell the reporters that you are not in favour of gambling and that the winning ticket was a gift from God ... unearned ... and that it really isn't yours, but a means to ease the needs of the poor, the homeless, addicts, and the unemployed."

Joseph was smiling from ear to ear. "Go on David, a servant is listening!"

"Then tell the press that you will be establishing a benevolent foundation ... you can challenge the audience for a name for the new organization. All the money, the $2,000,000, will be available for charity and worthy causes. And, in the process, challenge future winners to do the same thing with their so-called lucky wins. You, in so doing, will sermonize a homily of action, rather than mere words. It will astound the consumer culture and delight Christian believers. And make sure that they take a good number of pictures of you. We've got to choose a good one to make certain that you appear more handsome than you really are," teased David.

"Brilliant, David. Brilliant! A modern day adaptation of our Lord's parable of the three servants and the talents is recorded in Matthew

25:28. The servant who buried his talent was condemned by Jesus when He concluded the parable with the words, 'Take the talent from him and give it to him who has the ten talents.'

Christians who have means to do good are never to bury the opportunity to do so."

"Now that you are temporarily a rich man Joseph, how about buying a second cup of coffee?" needled Barclay.

"Glad to do it gentlemen! But don't get used to it! After I collect the $2,000,000 and set up the trust fund, I'll be back to being a poor, retired parish priest just like you two."

As Barclay drove home from the time with his two fellow clerics, his mind was racing. He had come with the intent of seeking topics for exploration to be fleshed out and submitted as editorials in the *Tangleville Mirror*. The Spirit had led him in a totally different path than he had planned to pursue.

"I don't know where I'm being led," he concluded. "But there must be topics to submit buried in Fr. Joseph's perceived dilemma."

The question that troubled him the most was how he would have personally handled Fr. Joseph's Christmas card with the gifted lottery ticket inside. Would he do as Joseph planned to do and give the money away? As a married man, he decided it was best to put the question to Faith. What really concerned him was in spite of his politically proclaimed stance of condemning lotteries, what would he really do if he were holding the winning ticket?

Would materialism trump his religious convictions?

Maybe a future submission for the *Tangleville Mirror* was in its stage of incubation.

Chapter Ten

STEADMORE'S meeting with his two cleric friends didn't end with the critters and coffee. Fr. Joseph's dilemma continued to resonate in his re-thinking of what it means to be an authentic Christian in this early twenty-first century. "Have we moderns been too easily grafted into the accepted secular ways of our time?" he wondered. "If St. Paul were with us in the flesh today, would he not be displeased with how there often seems to be little difference between the two 'V's' ... virtue and vice... in the general Christian population?"

It was now Thursday following the clerics' meeting and Barclay was convinced that he needed to address the issue. "Why not write an article for the *Tangleville Mirror*? If I am concerned about the easy accommodation of Christians nowadays to what once was deemed to be an anathema to the early churches' teachings of Christ, surely I am not alone," he reasoned.

The title for his article seemed to perfectly address his scepticism!

FROM (ST.) PAUL TO PABLUM?

Does Father Know Best?

by The Rev. Canon Dr. Barclay Steadmore

To refresh your memory, Pablum is a processed cereal for infants, invented by the Mead Johnson Company in 1931 through the work of Canadian pediatricians Frederick Tisdall, Alan Brown, and Theodore Drake. The root word for Pablum is the Latin word "pabulum," meaning "foodstuff." While Pablum is palatable and easily digested by babies, it has come to be referred to as bland, mushy, unappetizing … infantile … great for the very youngs' transition to be replaced by more desirable, tasty enjoyable food … steak and lobster, if you will! Pablum was and is designed for beginners in life, not as the main menu for a lifetime.

There is a time for Pablum in everyone's life, and a time to move on to digest more solid nourishment. Such is the case as well in one's transition from being a spiritual baby in Christ to maturing as an authentic faithful adult, living out the teachings of the Lord Jesus. St. Paul, in his first letter to the church in Corinth, Chapter 3:1-3 wrote: "And so, brothers and sisters, I could not speak to you as spiritual people, but rather as people of the flesh, as infants in Christ. I fed you with milk, not solid food, for you were not ready for solid food. Even now you are still not ready, for you are still of the flesh."

In today's language, St. Paul is saying: "Christians, move from a Pablum faith to the solid tenets of the Gospels."Theologians are well aware that modern Christianity is trending towards becoming labelled as "consumers" of Jesus, where individual believers customize what they find attractive in the Gospels and ignore what they find objectionable. Many, to be comfortable in a congregation, seek out a church where the message proclaimed from the pulpit makes one feel comfortable. Such churches seldom challenge the laity to grow beyond freewill individualism and self-serving, private personal structures.Austen Ivereigh, a British writer and journalist, in his book *The Great Performer*, referring to Pope Francis, quotes him calling our age "a culture of comfort" which makes us think only of ourselves, makes us insensitive to the cries of other people." In Pope Frances' words we hear the echo of the prophet Isaiah when he pleads with Israel to "Comfort, O comfort my people, says your God" (Isaiah 40:1). "But, why go to church?" asks the average citizen of this age. "I'm not comfortable in being told to reconsider the destructive powers of the world which disenfranchises the poor, the homeless, the unemployed. I've got enough of my own problems to address. I come first before those who cry for help. After all, didn't Jesus say: "For you always have the poor with you?" (Matt. 26:11)

So modern "consumer Christianity" prefers a Pablum diet of comfortable, easily digested menu of Sunday morning worship settings where a cozy church is good enough. It's really "designer Christianity" where the pew sitter determines what one wants to hear, and chooses a church where his or her needs are Pablum fed.

But such a cozy church proclaiming such self-serving theology is not good enough. In the Holy Scriptures over and over again we understand that the expression "it's not about you" becomes God proclaiming that true religion is "about others" as well as the self. There is a balance between one's personal relationship with God, and one's outwardly focus on humanity ... its needs, the poor, the sick, the disenfranchised ... even on all kinds of political issues. In so doing, "Pablum faith" is left behind and "spiritual meat" becomes the mature Christian's menu.

It comes as a shock for many modern Christians to come to the realization that we are all sinners. All have personal needs. But all humanity is in need of God's grace and all believers are instruments in addressing the wants of humankind. We all stand before God empty-handed on the merits of God's grace alone.

Thus, is modern Christianity, in many ways, a baby faith? Thinking theologians believe so. Why? Because:

1. Bible illiteracy is a major problem in the world;

2. Christians are aware of the concept of God's "grace" in the New Testament, but many dismiss the necessity of "works" in the daily life of everyday Christian living (see James 1:22-25 and 2:17);

3. Of the lack of understanding of the necessity of sacramental life. The centrality of the Holy Eucharist in the early church, the anointing of the sick, penance, fasting, and so forth;

4. The temptation to reinvent or reinterpret long-held theological doctrine, like marriage of same-sex couples, pre-marital sex, abortion, ease of divorce, and so forth.;

5. The ease of "church shopping" where one finds a theology that fits

one's personal desires ... to complement "self-fulfillment" rather than being challenged to focus on the "needs of others" ... The "me" versus "thee" centre of being;

6. The absence of the word "sin" in public worship;

7. Consumer worship where one attends church to "get something" rather than to pay over "spiritual taxes: to God;

8. Distrust of authority, in the Holy Scriptures, Tradition, the Early Church Fathers, and so forth; and

9. Anti-intellectualism: failing to understand that God in blessing the world has revealed truth in vastly different ways.

First through the Holy Scriptures (revealed truth); secondly through the incarnation (the gift of Christ, God's Son); and in later times through science (physics, mathematics, medicine, philosophy, psychology, astronomy, and so forth). Each in its own way reveals the glory of God. One does not contradict the other.

drsteadmore@starmail.com

Barclay was mentally exhausted! Shutting down his Mac, he decided it was time to see if Faith would like to take a short walk to the close-by bakery and coffee shop for a mid-morning break.

Faith was only too willing to go! Besides, he was anxious to spend some time with her because she had hinted at breakfast that something was on her mind. Knowing her uncanny ability to predict events in life, he over the years had come to the belief that she possessed a gift that he would never have. "Let's go Faith, I'm all ears to hear what's on your mind."

Chapter Eleven

It was only a three-block walk to the Sip and Savour Bake Shop. Barclay and Faith bundled up in winter parkas. They held gloved hands as they trudged through the last evening's four-centimetre snowfall. Traffic was light and it only took ten minutes to arrive at their destination.

Faith ordered a small regular coffee with double cream and a toasted bagel with cream cheese. Barclay settled for a medium dark roast, double cream, and a blueberry critter. As Barclay waited for their order to be filled, Faith went ahead and claimed two comfortable chairs in front of the electric fireplace.

They both sipped coffee as they savoured their chosen snacks. Barclay was interrupted twice by people who came over to say hello, telling him how much they were enjoying his submissions to the *Tangleville Mirror*. Apparently, relatives in Tangleville had cut out Barclay's articles and mailed them to their friends in Trinity Harbour.

"Why don't you also publish in our town's newspaper?" one lady asked.

Barclay explained that he had an exclusive contract with the Tangleville paper that prevented him from publication in competitive media. "But," smiling, Barclay advised them, "you are free to pass on your mailed copies to friends and neighbours. That will certainly be beyond my control, or the control of the *Tangleville Mirror*."

After the couple left, Faith grinned at Barclay.

"Always the consummate promoter, aren't you?"

"I'm not going there Faith! Let's talk about what you hinted at during breakfast. What is bothering you?"

"I can't get Harry and Annie out of my mind lately. Have you been in touch with either of them in the last month or so?"

"Now that you mention it, I haven't. What has got you so concerned?"

"Somehow or another, I think Harry is in need of someone to talk to. I think that his new position on town council may be more problematic than he first thought it would be. I think that he may be a little hesitant … maybe too proud to admit it."

"What do you think we should do to find out Faith? I can't simply call him and pry into what he may be concerned with. After all, your psychic intuitiveness is merely speculation. Harry is a big boy! Don't you think that if he wanted my counsel he would call me … or at least send an e-mail?"

Faith, in her diplomatic, tactful fashion that had been cultivated over the years, offered a thoughtful suggestion.

"Why don't we reserve a couple of nights at one of Tangleville's motels … take a trip to our old town and make a date when we get there with Harry and Annie? You can always tell the Stings that your contract with the *Tangleville Mirror* needs to be fine-tuned, thereby justifying the trip to our old haunt. If Harry wants or needs to confide in you for advice, let him open up the conversation."

"I like it Faith. I've got a couple of submissions yet to complete for the *Mirror*. When we get home, I'll begin work on them and take them to Tangleville with us. In the meantime, why don't you try to find a reasonably priced motel for a couple of nights … let's say for a Thursday and a Friday night? I know that Harry has his council meetings on Tuesdays and the mid-week celebration of the Eucharist here at St. Mary's is on Wednesday. I don't want to miss the Wednesday service. It is my spiritual boost that gets me from Sunday to Sunday."

"I'll take a look at the long-range weather forecast for the next couple of weeks, Bark. If the weather looks OK for travelling, I'm on. I'd like to do a little shopping with Annie at the Tangleville Mall. That will leave you some private time with Harry."

They finished their coffee, suited up for the cold walk back to their condo, and exited the bakery. Barclay hadn't noticed that a woman had waited for the two of them to go outside, and quickly followed them to the sidewalk.

"Excuse me, Dr. Steadmore! Can I interrupt you for a few minutes? I'll try to be brief!"

The lady didn't wait for Barclay to reply to her question.

"I've been reading your articles from the *Tangleville Mirror*, sent to me by my married daughter there."

"What's your name?" Barclay inquired.

"Carrie Spencer … I'm a member of the largest fundamentalist church here in Trinity Harbour. Our pastor insists that our denomination is the only true church. Can he be right?"

Before Barclay could answer, she continued. "Will you write an article for the Tangleville paper addressing such a claim? I want to give our minister a copy of your column. I don't have the theological background, nor the courage to personally confront him. Thank-you for listening." She hurried away before Barclay could introduce his wife to her, or to even give her an answer of "yes" or "no" to write such an article.

Faith squeezed Barclay's hand as they restarted their journey back to their home. "Well Dr. Steadmore, another of your fans, I see!" … the coy smile of hers giving away that she was teasing.

"I can't say right now Faith. But she certainly has provided me with a possible topic to pursue for a future column. Sorry I didn't get the opportunity to introduce you to her."

"She didn't want to meet me, that was obvious," Faith replied, as she gripped his gloved hand even more tightly.

Barclay, in his wisdom, decided not to go there.

Chapter Twelve

RETURNING to their condo, Barclay hurried to his study to work on a topic that he had been wrestling with for years. He was, in his mind, finally ready to try to tackle the age old problem: Why do bad things happen to good people?

I NEVER PROMISED YOU A ROSE GARDEN

Does Father Know Best?

by The Rev. Canon Dr. Barclay Steadmore

Do you remember the country song recorded by Lynn Anderson back in October of 1970, entitled "Rose Garden"? It was written by Joe South, first released in 1967 by Billy Joe Royal, but Anderson made it a national hit. This dates me of course, but back then everyone was singing or humming the tune. Most people referred to it by a longer title: "I Never Promised You a Rose Garden." The lyrics attempt to convey that a lover's relationship involves both good times and bad … the sunshine with the rain. Life is never easy. The song goes on to state that one can overcome adversity if the will exists.

Every time I hear those opening words, a theological message comes to mind. I'm certain that Joe South, the writer, didn't have theology motivating him to pen his words, but theology is there. Let me explain!

We've all heard it over and over: "Why would a loving God, all-knowing, all-powerful, all-compassionate, allow bad things to happen to so-called good people?"

Surely the popular logic of the age, suffering, need, pain, sickness, and mental anguish are terrible. Why does God permit such hardships to exist?

It is not only a Christian question. In 1981, Rabbi Harold Kushner published his now classic answer. Entitled "When Bad Things Happen to Good People," his work brought comfort to millions of readers. I advise all Christians to obtain a copy and read it.

Yet, the question of pain and suffering is one of the most difficult questions in all of theology.

Maybe the only honest answer that we humans can offer is that God has His own reasons. We, as mere humans, can only speculate as to what those reasons are. However, as followers of Christ and rational people, we can at least try to be conscious of where our reason falls short. Faith is sufficient to trust in God's benevolence, His love, and His grace.

Of course, this is not acceptable to critics of Christianity who respond that God is not all-good, all-knowing, or all-powerful. We Christians over the centuries have developed broad answers as to why the critics are wrong.

The secularists ask the thought-provoking question: "If God is real and in control, why does He allow natural disasters to occur: earthquakes, floods, tsunamis, volcanic eruptions, hurricanes? What about famine, world-wide epidemics … the list goes on … cancer, heart attacks, leukemia, AIDS?"

On the surface, these seem to be fair questions. If God really is a loving God, and is all powerful, is He not concerned about suffering and hardship? Could He not have prevented the Holocaust, the kidnapping of an innocent child, the slow painful death of an innocent person on their deathbed? Again, fair questions.

It needs to be said again: God has His own reasons. Humans do not know the full mind of God.

As Lynn Anderson's lyrics put it, it is as God has said to humanity: "I never promised you a rose garden."

Modern science has taught us that some evil results from free choices. If you stand too close to a fire, you may get burned. If you choose to swim in a swiftly flowing river, you run the risk of drowning. If you abuse your body with alcohol, street drugs, an unhealthy diet, and refuse to properly exercise, one cannot blame God … one has chosen to gamble with the consequences of choice.

Some evil comes from choosing to do nothing: driving while over the legal blood alcohol limit, not pulling over when you know you are too sleepy to continue further.

The opposite is equally true. Some evil results from the free choice of others: thefts, a drunk driver killing an innocent person, child abuse.

If an airplane crashes, can one blame God, or is it a matter of a multitude of possible reasons … improper maintenance, pilot error, sudden unpredicted weather? After all, most aircrafts do not crash. But some do. Is the latter God's fault?

Amusement rides sometimes fail. The wrong medicine is sometimes mistakenly given to patients. A horse kicks its owner. A pet bites its master. God's fault?

The critic would say, "But if God exists and is a loving God, He would stop it and prevent all of the above!"

Christians know that God sometimes intervenes and at times does not. So what could God possibly be revealing to us if He does not intervene?

I am convinced it is this: We have been created as freewill humans, not robots! If God had not created humans to possess the ability to make moral judgments, to indeed freely make choices, then human beings would be nothing more than puppets with God pulling the strings. Robots cannot sin! If humans do not have the capacity to sin, then there would be no need of a Saviour. Responsibility, accountability and conscience would not enter into the picture. Is that what we really want to be … Robots? … Puppets? Not existing as freewill agents who must choose or not to choose to live life aware of the consequences of free-choice decisions. I think not!

Well, we can't have it both ways!

The Holy Scriptures show us that some free choices of evil prompt moral development and meaning. Joseph's brothers sold him into slavery, but in so doing, "God meant it for good in the end."

Job was allowed to suffer terrible agony when God bet Satan that his servant would not curse his creator. Job argued with God, received no answers for his pleadings, yet in spite of it all, did not curse God. In the end, God restored Job to health, but Satan was taught the most important lesson for all time ... that in the end God wins! Job didn't know what was going on, but "God" in doing so, "had His reasons."

St. Paul in Romans 8:28 wrote: "We know that all things work together for good for those who love God, who are called according to his purpose."

Secular critics will scoff at St. Paul's statement, but Christians argue that pain, suffering, distress, and so forth are preparations for a greater life to come. Christians accept that pain awakens us to God and thus to the suffering of others ... that life on this earth is only a precursor of that real life that hasn't yet begun.

In the meantime, because of suffering and pain, new medicines, new drugs, yet undiscovered surgical techniques are on the horizon. Freewill agents, because of suffering and adversity, therefore, have the sacred privilege to intervene and participate in God's creation. What trust is granted to humans! Robots and puppets would never be granted the liberty of being co-creators with God! Yes, suffering in the mind of God has a purpose with meaning.

We may not know why in the fullest fashion, but God has His reasons for the ups and downs of human existence.

In the meantime, until God's will is complete, remember it is as Lynn Anderson almost put it: "God never promised us a rose garden." Rather, ours, in faith, is to tend the garden, for Jesus said in Matthew 28:20:

"And remember, I am with you always, to the end of the age."

drsteadmore@starmail.com

Chapter Thirteen

BARCLAY couldn't dismiss Faith's concerns about Harry's possible problems on Tangleville's town council. Time and time again, her predictions had proven to materialize. During the early years of their long marriage, Barclay would tease his wife about making up seemingly unlikely situations.

"Faith," he would say, "you have an overactive imagination. There is no evidence that your premonitions are true. I don't want to hear any more of your unconfirmed apprehensions!"

But time and time again Faith's intuitions proved to be accurate. As the years passed by, Barclay without actually admitting it to Faith, began to put more faith in what she seemed to be able to pick up as fact before learning the details of the event.

"Faith, I'm going to call James Parker's office and see if I can make an appointment to update my arrangement with the *Tangleville Mirror*. I'm going to suggest this coming Thursday morning. Will you check to see if you can reserve three nights at one of the Tangleville motels? That will allow us to check in during the early afternoon and call the Stings to invite them out for a dinner together. If we don't bunk in at the motel first, Annie will insist that we stay with them. I don't want to put them to the pressure of getting ready for guests, especially if Harry has obligations or council work that will take him away from quality time with us. If your premonition about Harry is correct, I'm certain that he and I will need to spend some serious time together."

Faith was quick to get online to try to book a Thursday, Friday, Saturday reservation. It would be the perfect opportunity to checkout of the motel on Sunday morning and attend morning worship at St. Bart's. It didn't take long for her to arrange the three night stay at the Welcome 2U Lodge.

"Barclay, we've got three nights reserved. Hope you have it worked out with Parker at the *Mirror*."

"James Parker has agreed to the meeting for Thursday at

11:00 a.m. Perfect timing for us! We can leave early that morning for the 110 miles to town and have a light breakfast on the way. I am excited about the trip! We haven't seen the Stings since Harry's swearing-in ceremony. I miss that couple! Maybe Annie will give me a ride in her '72 Jaguar XKE!"

"Maybe," teased Faith, "if there will be any time left over from the two of us doing the shopping circuit!"

Barclay knew that the "us" did not include himself. That "us" would certainly be Annie and Faith!

It was already late on Monday morning and Barclay decided that he had better retreat to his office and start to write another article for the *Tangleville Mirror*. With a freshly brewed cup of coffee in hand, he settled down before his Mac and logged on. It would be a good idea, he reasoned, to hand James Parker his next submission while he was with the editor in person. The topic had been percolating in his mind for some weeks. Now was the perfect time to flesh it out, especially since James could read the title in Barclay's presence. "It would be interesting," Barclay reasoned, "to watch for a facial expression to give away approval or rejection of the yet unwritten words." The title of Barclay's submission would certainly be troubling to the paper's secular readership who claims to be free from religious restrictions!

PROVE TO ME THAT YOU ARE NOT RELIGIOUS!
Does Father Know Best?
by The Rev. Canon Dr. Barclay Steadmore

Modern secular society takes great pride in stressing that it is free from the restrains of organized religion ... Christianity, Judaism, Islam, to name the major religions in the world.

Webster's dictionary defines religion as "an organized system of beliefs, rites, and celebrations centered on a supernatural being power; belief pursued with devotion."

Set aside that last definition for a moment: "belief pursued with devotion."

The Thesaurus further explains the concept of belief. It states: "The act of assenting intellectually to something proposed as true or the state of mind of one who assents."

I submit that being "religious" has at least two ways of being interpreted.

The first contains the standard elements of organized religion: a gathering community where a belief system, rituals, ethics, emotional experiences, and sacramental observances take place, all based upon a recognized central authority of sacred writings and tradition. Members are expected to attend and participate in such gatherings on a regular basis, thus fulfilling the definition: "The act of assenting intellectually to something proposed as true or the state of mind of one who assents."

Atheists, agnostics, and lapsed members of any religious body who do not adhere to nor practice the above, therefore claim that they are "non-religious." For such people, this non-adherence is claim for personal freedom and self-determination in all so-called "divine" realities!

Such people proudly claim to adhere to Karl Marx's famous quote:

"Religion is the sigh of the oppressed creature, the heart of the heartless word, and the soul of the soulless conditions. It is the opium of the people."

But I submit that to be religious involves an additional interpretation, one that manifests in every human being, making every individual a religious entity. Why? Because all humans are designed to be religious. One cannot help but be religious because, it's basic to the human condition!

The above critics of organized religions scoff at such a statement! But let me propose a straightforward, all inclusive, modern definition of "being religious":

"To be religious is to surrender one's life to whatever gives supreme meaning ... whatever such devotion may cost that human being."

In our age, a classic reversion from monotheism to polytheism has taken place. Individuals now feel free to create their own "gods" ... small "g" required, and to forfeit the cost of doing so to whatever the price of adherence of such worship should require.

A multitude of twenty-first century "gods" now demand their own forms of worship: success, status, financial independence, the "in" dress code, living in a status neighbourhood, political correctness, membership in an elite club, the worship of physical fitness, and the perfect body. The list continually grows!

Don't tell me that each of the above "gods" does not demand religious adherence ... even regular devotion to maintain such dominance in its individual and/or congregational membership. There now exists legions of "gods" to which one may surrender one's soul!

And people willingly do and thus religiously adhere to one's self-invented religion!

We live in a "Harry Potter world" where the appeal of the novel's centre on magic and the supernatural. If the people do not accept the reality of the "divine," they are most able and willing to create such imagined beings and bow down to them. Case in point! In spite of confessing to being non-religious, one religiously may surrender to superstitions of all kinds. Superstition by its nature, infers that power exists beyond human existence ... that what is may be altered.

Otherwise, why would one be advised to cross one's fingers ... not to open an umbrella in the house ... believe in fortune telling ... avoid crossing over the path of a black cat ... horoscopes ... ghosts ... magic ... knocking on wood ... wishing one another "good luck" ... all the way to believing in casting of spells and carrying a four-leaf clover or a rabbit's foot?

The one that seems most puzzling to Christians is why a non-believer in Jesus Christ as the Son of God would be superstitious and fearful of Friday the 13th. One theory for the origin of that superstition centres on the story of Jesus' last supper and crucifixion in which thirteen individuals were present in the Upper Room on the 13th of Nisan, Maundy Thursday, the night before Christ's death on Good Friday. Fact or not, this date seems to be of interest to superstitious people. Why would non-believers in God's Son pay any attention to such an event?

Why? Because just below the surface of every human being lies the built-in nature to reach beyond the self to some power in control of what one cannot control.

Religions use "acts" to perform rituals which express or represent beliefs. Ritual is really an attempt to conform to doing what is advantageous in the mind of the doer.

Why do people religiously put one leg in one's trousers before the other? Or habitually tie one shoe before the other? Brush one's teeth on the same side before crossing over to the other side ... time after time? Humans are not only creatures of habit, but religiously so in nature. In so doing, rituals are ways to make sense of one's beliefs to fit together in a system which integrates the self into the universe. In so doing, one can live out, even creating, one's personal religion.

I have never yet met a person who is not religious, for one's beliefs are revealed, made real through ceremonies. Dr. Jordan Peterson, the clinical psychologist states, "You can only find out what you believe ... rather than what you think you believe ... by watching how you act."

In simple terms, to be religious is to habitually submit one's life over to the pursuit of whatever one considers to give the most significant goal to achieve personal fulfillment ... whatever the cost and sacrifice is needed to do so ... Webster's dictionary statement "belief pursued with devotion" fulfilled!

So non-religious claimers, identify your "god" or "gods" you worship! Are you monotheistic or polytheistic in your secular state of being human? Bowing down to one "god" or to many?

drsteadmore@starmail.com

Barclay closed down his Mac. He smiled to himself wondering how Tangleville's readership would respond. "Better be sure to remind Parker to forward to me all the Letters to the Editor which will surely follow this publication," mused Barclay. "I can't wait to read them!"

Chapter Fourteen

BARCLAY and Faith arose early on Thursday morning. The meeting with James Parker was set for 11:00 a.m. and the couple planned to get away by 7:15 a.m. to enjoy a leisurely drive to Tangleville. They had packed their luggage the night before and Barclay had checked the oil in the Mustang to make sure it was topped up for the trip. Even though the red convertible was not an oil consumer, old habits formed from driving older high mileage used cars during their first years of marriage when cars burned and leaked oil. Barclay never set out on a longer trip without performing the ritual to set his mind at ease. His father used to say, "Oil is cheaper than repairs."

Stopping at the local drive-through, they picked up their morning coffee … Faith a regular with one cream, and he a dark roast with double cream. It was a beautiful warm morning and they decided to lower the convertible top to enjoy the morning sunshine. Faith wore a bright red kerchief to protect her hair which would otherwise be windblown, and Barclay sported a plaid newsboy driving cap.

"Two old fogies out together!" Faith quipped to Barclay.

Forty-five minutes into their trip they turned into the Hi Way Diner, for a breakfast break. The lot was filled with pick-up trucks, a clue to the Steadmores that the locals considered the diner a favourite spot to stop off and gather. Barclay parked next to a 4x4 black Toyota Tundra, pushed the button to raise the convertible's top, and locked the car. The large seating area was almost filled and after reading the sign at the entrance that read "Seat Yourself," they located a table for two near the rear of the restaurant.

A busy waitress, coffee in hand, approached their table, asked if they wanted coffee and whether or not they needed a menu. It certainly was a noisy atmosphere and it seemed that everyone appeared to know each other.

"I think we've made a good choice Faith," Barclay, in a low voice, spoke above the din of the crowd.

Faith nodded as she quickly perused the well-worn menu, and then looking up at the breakfast specials written on the chalkboard to her left, said, "I'm going to have pancakes and the fruit selection. What about you?"

"I can't turn down the two eggs and corn beef hash deal." He barely got the words out of his mouth and the waitress was at their table.

"What will it be," she demanded. She wasn't about to spend unwanted conversation before she hurried over to the kitchen window and placed the two orders. She didn't even write down the orders. She simply shouted it to the short order cook on the other side of the serving window. In exactly eleven minutes, their orders were slid across their plastic tablecloth and the efficient waitress disappeared.

It was a most delicious breakfast in spite of the lack of attractive decor surrounding the crowded room and the no-nonsense attention of the waitressing staff. Following a refill of their coffee cups, their bill was tossed onto their table and aware that another couple was waiting for a table, Barclay and Faith made their way to the cashier to pay their fare.

As they walked to their red Mustang, Faith squeezed Barclay's hand and said, "That was refreshing, wasn't it? It is so great to see people enjoying one another's company and the lack of feigned pretentions. Let's stop in here again on our return to Trinity Harbour."

"It's fine with me, Faith. Do we put the top down for the rest of the trip, or leave it up?"

"Leave it up! We may be a little behind time for you to meet with Parker. We can make better time with the top closed. Besides, I don't want to get windblown. I just went for a hair shampoo and cut yesterday."

Barclay knew better than to argue the point. They arrived in Tangleville at 10:45 a.m. and pulled up in front of the *Tangleville Mirror* offices. Barclay handed Faith the keys to the car and asked her to keep her cell phone on. He would call her when his appointment with Parker was over and she could then pick him up where they are now parked.

"I'm going over to my former favourite dress store, Bark. Give me a ring when you are ready. I've got my Visa card!" She smiled that coy smile of hers when she said that.

Barclay approached the reception desk to announce his arrival.

"Yes, Doctor. Mr. Parker is expecting you. He will greet you in a few minutes."

Barclay took a comfortable large leather chair just to the left of the waiting area and sat down. Copies of the *Tangleville Mirror* were sitting on the table to his right and he sorted through the pile to find the one that contained his last submission, "I Never Promised You a

Rose Garden." The edition that he really wanted to find was the one with letters to the editor so that he could scan the letters to see how readers were reacting to the article.

Before he was able to do so, James Parker came rushing to greet him.

"Good Morning, Doctor! Great to see you. Samantha is waiting in my office. Would you like a cup of coffee?"

"No thanks, Mr. Parker. Maybe a little later if our time together is extended." Barclay was hoping that his answer might convey to James that there could be serious topics to pursue and that they might require some extra time to sort them out.

"Call me James, Doctor. I'm looking forward to our time together!"

Barclay followed James to his large impressive office and Samantha rose to greet him, her hand out to grasp his.

"Welcome Doctor! It's been some time since we last met in this office. How have you been? And your spouse, Faith?"

Barclay quickly sensed that he was receiving a warm welcome. "Things must be going OK as far as his submissions are concerned," he thought to himself. Now, to wait for the appropriate opportunity to bring up his concerns.

Each sat in comfortable black leather chairs around a large coffee table in the room. After about five minutes of polite small talk, James opened the door for conversation about the real reason for Barclay's visit.

"How would you say that our agreement is working out, Doctor?" As expected, Samantha let James lead the conversation.

Barclay responded to Parker's question with his own inquiry. "First, let's begin with your assessment as to how your readership is reacting to my columns … general agreements, violent opposition, or worse yet, general complacency?"

"Certainly not your third apprehension, Doctor! We've had more letters to the editor following each of your submissions than to any of the articles in our publications. Yours arouses more submissions than we expected. Keep those submissions coming!"

"All right then, what would you say is the split between letters of support and those who disagree?"

Samantha spoke up. "I'd say two-thirds in agreement and one-third inordinately opposed."

"And how does that split fit into your expectations of what should be happening," responded Barclay.

"That is about right as it is now! We know that positive responses over opposition to articles are good for the newsprint business. The more pointed a submission is by the writer, the more letters to the editor we are likely to receive."

"Tell me about letters you have received to date. What would you say would be an expected number following each of my submissions?"

"Oh, we get them all right!" smiled Samantha. Your submissions usually get thirty letters per article. We can only publish about two per day. That is about all the room the editorial section will allow, since there are other topics from readers we must also consider. We, however, keep a copy of all letters received in our archives."

This was now Barclay's opening he had been waiting for. "James and Samantha, when we shook hands on our agreement for me to submit articles, it was my understanding that I would be receiving copies of all letters to the editor. To date, I have received only those letters that have been published in later editions. I really would appreciate reading those that you considered not worthy to publish. Can that be arranged in the future?"

James looked over at Samantha and Barclay noticed that she gave him an almost undetectable nod in the affirmative.

"Doctor," James responded. "We never do that kind of thing for other writers in our paper, but I think in your case we can send you copies, which we would then ask you to return to us on your future visits to our office. We will, of course, keep accurate records of those we send. Is that agreeable to you?"

"That is perfect! The reason I want to read the submitted responses is to get a better understanding of how to address future submissions … What people are thinking … What interests them when they oppose my ideas!

"And there is another question I wish to follow up with. You will remember that I refused an honorarium for my work, but instead asked you to send donations to the Samaritan Inn to help out with their organization. Can you give me an idea of how that has been going?"

Samantha opened her Mac notebook and quickly found the information for Barclay. "Dr. Steadmore, to date we have sent them cheques totalling $800. We have the receipts to verify these numbers."

"I'm very pleased, Samantha. I have a soft spot for the good work that they do."

"Anything else, Doctor?" asked James.

"Yes, I've brought with me the submission for the next publication date. Do you care to take a quick look at the contents?"

James looked over the manuscript and Barclay looked for telltale facial expressions on the editor's face as he quickly read the article entitled "Prove To Me That You Are Not Religious!"

There was silence in the room until James put down the article and extended his open hand to Barclay.

"Perfect! I can't wait for the letters to the editor to follow. I know some people in town who are going to be quite upset with your work. Keep these types of topics coming!"

"Thanks James. Oh, there is one tiny item to address. It is about 110 miles from Trinity Harbour to Tangleville. I'll be pleased if you would cut a cheque to cover my expenses here and back home."

James and Samantha rose to their feet to shake hands with Barclay, and both walked him to the front desk.

"We'll take care of your mileage, Doctor. Come to visit us as often as you can. We really appreciate having you on staff. Our greetings to Faith!"

Barclay stepped outside onto the sidewalk to call Faith to pick him up. To his surprise, she was parked just across the street, the top down on the Mustang.

"Well Bark, how did it go?"

"I'm really hungry, Faith. Let's find a drive-through restaurant and I'll fill you in. By the way, how was your shopping spree?"

"There is still room on the Visa card for more," she grinned. She slid the shift lever into drive and the rear tires gave an audible chirp.

Barclay didn't utter a single word in response. He was a lucky man to have her as his wife. Faith knew what he was thinking as she reached over and gave him a light tap on the cheek. There was very little that he could withhold from his intuitive spouse.

Chapter Fifteen

FOLLOWING a quick lunch at a local burger joint, Faith behind the wheel pulled into the parking lot of the Welcome 2U Lodge. Since she had made the reservations for the three-night stay in Tangleville, Faith parked the Mustang and hurried into the lobby to book in.

It only took about five minutes before she returned to their car, motel room door keys in hand. "Room 108 to the left of the building, Bark. We have a sliding door from our ground-floor room opening to the parking lot."

Barclay took the motel keys, hurried down the hall to room 108, unlocked the sliding door to the already parked Mustang outside, and together Faith and he carried in their luggage.

"I'm going to take a short nap, Faith. See if you can contact the Stings and arrange for us to take them out to dinner."

"Getting a little old, are you?" Faith teased. "Need your afternoon down time, as usual?"

He could hear Faith talking on her cell phone, but since he was one of those folks who could fall asleep in minutes, he dozed off for a thirty-minute snooze. When he awoke, Faith was in the bathroom applying fresh makeup.

"Well, how did you make out with the Stings?"

"Tonight won't work. Harry has a meeting to attend because he chairs the committee that lets out contracts for street maintenance, but tomorrow night is wide open. I set up the dinner date for 6:30 p.m. at the Tangleville Steak House. After dinner, we are invited to go over to the Stings' for dessert. How does all that sound?"

"Great! What do you want to do for the rest of the day?"

"Let's spend the rest of the afternoon on a tour out into the country. It's been a couple of years since we've done so. I'll even agree to put the top down on the Mustang!"

* * *

Friday morning was a bright, sunny, and warm day. After an enjoyable complimentary breakfast at the motel, they returned to their room for preparations for the rest of the day.

"What are you going to do today, Bark? Annie is picking me up at 9:30 a.m. for a shopping excursion and lunch together. The Mustang is all yours for the next few hours."

"I'm going to drive over to St. Bart's and see if I can take the rector out for coffee. After that, I'm coming back here to do some writing for my next submission to the *Tangleville Mirror*. Have fun together. Remember, we are going to have to pick up Harry and Annie around 6:10 p.m. in order to get to the restaurant in time for dinner. I'll confirm the reservations after I complete my morning devotions."

* * *

It was 12:30 p.m. after Barclay returned to Room 108 following his extended coffee meeting with Canon Matthew at St. Bartholomew's

Anglican Church. Barclay was delighted that after his successor took over at the parish, the congregation continued to be growing in numbers ... the sure sign of a healthy influential Christian presence in the community. Not being hungry after two cups of coffee and a large apple critter, he was anxious to sit down with his Mac and put words to paper.

TRADING GOD FOR GADGETS
Does Father Know Best?
by The Rev. Canon Dr. Barclay Steadmore

As one journeys through life, wise and fortunate is the individual who pauses to ask fundamental questions: questions one ought not to wait too late in life to ask. Such questions are certainly not new, but apply to every generation and have been posed, and more often than not, been left unanswered to the detriment of the self and society.

A survey of such questions include: What is the purpose of life? What brings true meaning and happiness in life? When is enough material gain enough?

Will my life make a difference in the future of the world? What am I doing right now that is making someone else's life a better one?

In a sense, all such questions are interrelated. Certainly, secular society will pose answers that are at odds with people of faith, particularly Christians. We, the citizens of the twenty-first century, have never been more aware of this fact. Materialism and the pursuit of self-gratification are proof of this observation.

Let's address the obsessive drive for material gain in our modern age. The flamboyant millionaire Malcolm Forbes is credited to have stated: "He who dies with the most toys wins." In our modern society driven by consumption, few will take exception to Forbes' claim. Why is this so? Why is materialism so routinely sought when its rewards are so fleeting?

It has been suggested that acquiring things becomes important when one has an inner void. When the inner void is deprived, external things are often chosen, sought after, to fill the emptiness of being. The void, however, is seldom diminished by doing so.

Possessions prized when first acquired, can bring immediate feelings of satisfaction. But such feelings of accomplishment soon evaporate and need to be replaced with another "fix." I call such possessions the "gadgets" of materialism! Psychologists know that gadgets have their own specific applications. But gadgets when not applied to specialized tasks need to be stored to be used only when the occasion arises for their intended usage. They, in their dormant state, are simply possessions! Things! Objects! Taking up storage room. Material possessions do not fill the inner need to be content! One can ask the question: Does the person own the possessions, or do the possessions own the person?

But what can fill this inner void? Certainly not 'things'!

The Funeral liturgy from the Book of Common Prayer reminds people of this fact. How often have you heard the words pronounced at the beginning of the service which state: "(For) we brought nothing into the world, so that we can take nothing out of it" (1 Timothy 6:7).

There is no need for pockets in caskets!

So, that which brings contentment, meaning, the balm to the inner void cannot be materialistic!

On the contrary: Service to others, personal challenges, the pursuit of knowledge, meaningful work, and mutual relationships do. All of these are the direct opposite to compulsive buying, being discontent with what we have, trying to "keep up with the Joneses," not enough space to store all our stuff (our gadgets), getting nervous and critical when the rector preaches for the need of stewardship, failing to give God the tithe which is His. In summary, materialism is the sin of thinking of the self as owners rather than managers, stewards of God's entrusted resources. In simple terms: trading God for gadgets. Christians, consider the following:

1. We are not the things we own! Let us separate our identities from what we possess;

2. Rather, it is putting God first in life, in relationships, and in service to others;

3. It is in becoming the Good Samaritan that brings inner peace and satisfies the inner void of being.

Materialism just doesn't cut it!

Voltaire said:

"The man who leaves money to charity in his will is only giving away what no longer belongs to him."

Bernard de Clairvaux put it this way:

"There is an endless road, a hopeless maze, [for those] who seek for goods before they seek for God."

Our Lord told His listeners this truth when he preached to those around Him:

"Do not store up for yourselves treasures on earth, where moth and rust consume and where thieves break in and steal; but store up for yourselves treasures in heaven ... For where your treasure is, there your heart will be also" (Matthew 6:19,21).

Those who have developed a healthy inner world will see possessions as merely neutral rather than being *chained* to things, gadgets, and material objects. God requires that we use what we have been blessed with to *unchain* and give liberty to those who are in want.

We Christians are in the world, but not of it!

drsteadmore@starmail.com

* * *

It was 5:30 in the afternoon when Barclay shut down his Mac. Faith's voice startled him as she came through the front entrance door.

"Are you ready to leave soon for the Stings'?"

"I'll be dressed in a few minutes, Faith. It has been a productive afternoon. I have another submission to the *Tangleville Mirror* completed."

Chapter Sixteen

THE Stings and the Steadmores arrived in the parking lot of the Tangleville Steak House five minutes before 6:30 p.m. All four were smartly attired and upon entering, they were met by the maître d'.

"Welcome folks. Your table is waiting."

It was obvious that Harry was now recognizable by many in town. His frequent pictures in the *Tangleville Mirror* had made him somewhat of a celebrity town councillor.

The waitress approached their table and greeted them with a warm smile.

"Great to see you again, Mr. Sting. I'm assuming that the attractive lady to your left is your spouse?"

Harry introduced Annie, Faith, and Barclay to Ginette, the waitress. She graciously led them to a table for four and placed the menus before each of them.

"I'll give you a few minutes to peruse our entrées. Will anyone be ordering something from the bar?"

It was like old times together in former years. Four close friends catching up on events in their lives. Even though the Stings and the

Steadmores regularly exchanged e-mails, it was so much more enjoyable to sit around a table and communicate in person.

Annie ordered a small steak, medium rare. Faith decided on roast beef and onions, her favourite choice. Harry and Barclay both decided on a large steak with mushrooms … Harry's well done and Barclay's medium rare. The choice of potato was either baked or mashed, and the vegetable was either a medley of peas, corn, and carrots or roasted cauliflower and broccoli. The service and the food were excellent.

Over tea and coffee following the main course, Barclay discreetly inquired of Harry as to how he was enjoying the new position of town councillor. A slightly detectable frown came over Harry's face.

"Well, Barclay, it is a minefield around that table during weekly meetings. Sometimes I feel that being behind the microphone at AM KNOW was a far more enjoyable job!"

Annie, undetectable to Barclay and Faith, kicked Harry under the table. Harry, after years of marriage, got the message.

"Let's not spoil our meal with unpleasant details," Harry responded to Barclay's question. "I'm having too great a time together with great friends!"

Barclay instantly recognized that when he and Harry could be alone together, he needed to pursue the matter of Harry's telltale response to his question.

Earlier in the afternoon when the two women were together, Annie had invited the Steadmores back to the house after the restaurant meal for dessert. After Barclay paid the bill and a 20% tip for Ginette, the four set off for the Sting residence, arriving at 8:45 p.m.

Annie and Faith retired to the living room for a time together and Harry motioned for Barclay to follow him downstairs to the den.

"I've got some new pieces of Annie's art to show you Barclay. I'm very proud of her latest masterpieces!"

"Dessert will be served in about a half hour, fellows. Will it be coffee or tea for you?"

"Coffee," replied Barclay. "Double cream."

"Tea, Annie," called out Harry.

Barclay waited for Harry to point out Annie's latest paintings, not yet available to the public. Once her patrons were to see them, they would be quickly purchased and never be in the Stings' possession again.

The two sat down in comfortable leather-bound chairs, and following ten minutes or so of small talk, Barclay decided to redirect their conversation with another similar but opened ended question which previously had gone unanswered at the restaurant.

"Harry, how are you making out as one of Tangleville's newest councillors?"

There was a long pause and Harry's facial expression turned to a frown.

"Barclay, I'm really not sure that I can, at times, carry on."

"Tell me about it, Harry. I'm listening."

"Perhaps I was rather naive when I decided to let my name be attached to that ballot last election day. If I would have known then what I know now, I'm not sure that I would do it again."

"Postmortems are always troubling, Harry. Let's talk about it!"

"Barclay, I'm having a crisis of conscience. There are times when my faith stances are being challenged. There seems to be so many occasions when morals conflict with easy, convenient, self-serving decisions. I'm being pressured from many sides to compromise my new-found Christian principles."

"Give me an example, Harry. Let's pursue your apprehensions one at a time."

"You know that I am the chair of the committee that reviews the applications for street paving in Tangleville. Currently, we have three contractors who have submitted sealed bids to win the contract. Of course, I can't tell you the names of the firms. All are highly qualified to win the bid. All three bids have arrived in my office, and all three vary by only a mere $4,000 ... so close that the council will have to take my recommendations as to which company gets the OK.

"Well, yesterday, one of the owners of one of the bidding firms arrived in my office requesting ten minutes of my time. I reluctantly gave the OK for a brief meeting. The owner and CEO, carrying a very expensive leather briefcase, sat down before me and tried verbally to twist my arm to recommend his firm for the contract. I listened, gave him a brief time to make his case, and did not in any way promise him special consideration for a win. He shook my hand, thanked me for listening, and left.

"Ten minutes after his departure, my secretary entered my office and commented, 'I see you have a new briefcase there in front of your desk.'

"I replied, 'Mary, I don't have a new briefcase. It must belong to the contractor that was here a few minutes ago. If there is no name on the outside, open it and see if it has any identifiable information inside.'

"It wasn't locked, Barclay. Mary opened it and inside was a single envelope addressed to me. I asked Mary to open it. Inside the envelope she discovered ten crisp new $100 bills! I directed Mary to call the contractor and come back to retrieve his forgotten suitcase. Mary was back within a ten-minute interval. She had contacted the contractor on his cell phone and he had told her that the briefcase was a gift for me."

"OK, Harry … what's the problem?"

Barclay knew where Harry was going, but he wanted his friend to supply the answer. The moral problem was his alone to solve.

"Barclay, for a few fleeting seconds, and I'm ashamed to admit it, I was tempted to say to Mary, 'Let's split the $1,000, evenly. Say nothing to anyone and we'll celebrate our windfall.' But I didn't say it, Barclay. Somehow my faith won out."

"So, what did you do, Harry?"

I told Mary to call a taxi and to drop off the briefcase and the letter to the office of the contractor. The secretary of the contractor's office called my office within thirty minutes to say that the briefcase and unopened letter, which I had sealed, were delivered."

"Well done, Harry. So, again, I ask you, what is the problem?"

"Barclay, I can't get it out of my mind! What if Mary had not been involved as a witness? Would I still have sent the briefcase back? Would I have had the moral strength not to keep the money and not tell anyone? Something like this is going to happen again, I'm sure! If one contractor felt it was all right, it is likely that it is a common practice for others!"

"Harry, the fact that you are confessing your concerns to me, tells me that your Christian faith is stalwart. You are, after all, a mere human being. All Christians have times of self-doubt. Introspection is absolutely a human condition. But the fact that you did what you did should be celebrated. You have already answered your own concerns!

Your convictions are so grounded in Christ that you don't need to doubt what you would do in future similar situations!"

"Barclay, there is another concern I have. I wasn't prepared for it when I first took my seat in council. The mayor has pet projects which he wishes to tackle … to fulfill parts of his campaign promises given before his election to the office. He has let it be known to me, always in private, that if I side with him on council when a vote comes up to pass his pet project motions, that he'll vote in favour of motions which I bring before council. But what if I don't feel that I can support one of his motions? Do I vote against my conscience? Again, what I know may be in opposition to the views of those who elected me in my ward?"

Barclay didn't respond to Harry's questions. Annie interrupted their conversation when she appeared with a serving tray with two large pieces of blueberry pie and the cups of ordered coffee and tea. Both Harry and Barclay sat back down together and savoured Annie's culinary skills … the pie was absolutely delectable!

Barclay was appreciative of Annie's interruption. It would give him a few minutes to formulate a response to Harry's latest concern as they enjoyed their desserts.

With the pie consumed, still savouring his coffee, he asked Harry the question: "Harry, when have you ever not been your own man?"

"What do you mean by that, Barclay?"

"When have you, especially in your former career as a radio host, ever allowed someone to intimidate you?"

"Well, I can't remember anyone doing that!"

"And when did you also not side with a caller when that person presented, in your view, a valid argument to a point on your program that you felt was correct, innovative, and thoughtful?"

"Yes, I did that time and time again!"

"What has changed now Harry in your role as a city councillor? Surely the mayor must at times be promoting motions worthy of your support. And surely there will arise some of his pet projects which you and your ward members cannot, in all good conscience, support. What has changed, Harry? Let your morals, your ethics, and your judgments be your criteria for your voting record. Not only will you be your own man in doing so, but you will be held in higher esteem by the mayor and the rest of the council members. Your ward members will love you in so doing!"

"I needed that, Barclay. Thank-you! Deep down inside, I guess that I really knew the answer. I never was and never will be for sale."

"Now I know that the Christmas season will be upon us in about six weeks. Let me pose a scenario that you may have to face, Harry."

"First, let me go upstairs and refill our cups and see if there are any leftover pieces of pie. When I come back, I'm all ears."

Harry was back in five minutes, the tray bearing refilled cups of coffee and tea and two more slices of Annie's pie.

"Harry, I've heard that there is a rule that town councillors are not to accept gifts from the public, especially gifts that could be interpreted as means of obligation to favour the gift-givers in future council discussions. Is that true?"

"It certainly is, Barclay."

"Suppose this Christmas Eve that you and Annie should discover that packages have been dropped off on your front porch ... no cards attached, but with a little detective work you discover that the containers of the gifts are imprinted with the names of the companies involved. It is not subtle, but clearly obvious. What do you and Annie do, Harry? Who will ever know if you just accept the gifts and never let on to anyone?"

"Bark!" It was Faith's voice at the top of the stairs. "It is getting late. We'd better let these folks get to bed. Are you ready to leave?"

"I'll think about it, Barclay, said Harry. I'll e-mail you in the near future with my answer. Thanks for everything tonight! You are a good friend."

Barclay and Harry gave each other a bear hug just before they ascended the stairs.

Barclay thought to himself, smiling inwardly, "It is always the same situation. I didn't need to preach to Harry or give him advice which he didn't already know. Such is the way it always is with faithful, committed Christians. A good councillor allows such clients to dig deep into one's spiritual self and formulate solutions which coincide with the Gospel principles. The Holy Spirit is ever-present and leading in life's challenges!"

Chapter Seventeen

THE return trip to Trinity Harbour was an enjoyable time for Barclay and Faith. A warm day permitted the top of the Mustang to be down and Faith wore a kerchief to protect her otherwise windblown hair. Barclay, wearing aviation style sunglasses, would now and then glance over at her and think to himself how beautiful she was. After all these years of marriage, he was still in love with her as much as he was when they made their wedding vows. They travelled long periods without conversation, just soaking up the sun, the wind and the sound of the big five litre V8 engine.

Thinking about his discussion with Harry the night before, Barclay felt it was time to congratulate Faith on her ability to sense insights into situations that he himself would never have even considered. Her proven psychic ability, many times in the past confirmed to be accurate, no longer really surprized him. Now he just assumed her predictions as most likely accurate and knew that he had better pay attention to her premonitions.

Halfway home, they again pulled into the Hi Way Diner. The parking lot was half filled with vehicles, confirming their suspicions that the stop-off place must be a favourite gathering place for locals and people who travelled the highway. Inside, they found a table for two and ordered coffee and muffins. After a washroom break, they continued on their way to Trinity Harbour. It was 1:30 p.m. when they arrived at their condo.

The weekend and the days following were again routine in nature. Worship on Sunday morning was always mandatory. Barclay looked forward to the new week to begin writing his next submission to the *Tangleville Mirror*. Faith usually did laundry on Mondays and shopping for groceries on Tuesdays.

* * *

Monday morning, a fresh cup of coffee in hand, Barclay retired to his office which he maintained in one corner of the spare bedroom. Turning on his Mac, he had already decided on the title for his next article. It was a topic that he had been wrestling with for a number of years: Tolerance.

TOLERANCE AND CHRISTIANITY

Does Father Know Best?

by The Rev. Canon Dr. Barclay Steadmore

In today's western cultures, tolerance has come to mean that if anyone or any group disagrees with secular society's definition of tolerance, such a group or individual exhibits bigotry. Secularism now claims that all views on religion are equally valid, and furthermore, today's insistence on such a claim leaves no room for objective moral judgements. That is, one religion's view is as good, as valid, and as equal to any other!

While Christians can be tolerant of many areas of secular life, they cannot accept this secular definition of religious tolerance!

Webster's dictionary defines the word "tolerate" to mean "to put up with; to recognize and respect the opinions and rights of others; to endure; to suffer."

Such a definition does not imply that all views are of equal acceptance. Tolerance is not styling the truth to make one's views more acceptable or agreeable to others. Tolerance loves others even when they don't adjust their views to the individual who disagrees with them. Respect for the other's view in no way implies acceptance of such views.

1 Peter 3:15-16 put it very clearly for Christians: "Do not fear what they fear, but in your hearts sanctify Christ as Lord. Always be ready to make your defence to anyone who demands from you an account of hope that is in you, yet do it with gentleness and reverence." This surely applies in our world of separation of religion and state where everyone has the right to express one's evaluation of religious views. One has by law the right to do so! But this does not mean that Christians must, or should accept such compelling views as equal to the teaching of Holy Scripture. We, as Christians, must tolerate or put up with such views, but in no way are we to integrate or graft contrary or opposing religious teachings into Christian doctrine or practice.

Christians have never interpreted Christ's teachings to be equal to any of the other many religions, just another spoke in the wheel with God at the hub. For Jesus said: "I am the way, and the truth, and the life. No one comes to the Father except through me" (John 14:6).

Christ made an exclusive statement. Christ was either right and correct in so stating, or He was misinformed. This second option is for Christians a moot argument. Therefore, Christians have no choice but to reject today's secular claim that all paths to God are of equal consideration.

True tolerance then entails that in a free society, Christians are obligated to "put up with" competing religions, but to do so with respect and gentleness. The truth of the Gospels is non-negotiable. Any "car guy" understands that while both are automobiles, a Camry is not a LADA!

Clement F. Rogers, in *Verify Your References*, said: "It is easy to be tolerant when you do not care."

Christians care about the truth of the message of Jesus Christ. In no way can Christians compromise the teachings of the New Testament.

Should Christians then be tolerant? Yes, in the classical sense, in the true meaning of the dictionary definition of the term. The good kind of tolerance, in our open society, welcomes free speech and views that differ.

Christians, however, must not merge opposing theological views into historic orthodox Christianity.

Tolerance for Christians, therefore, means loving others unconditionally, while allowing others to voice competing messages in all areas of being, especially when it comes to different beliefs about God, yet standing firm in matters of historic Biblical truth and doctrine.

This being said, Christians notwithstanding see all people as God's people … His creations … endowed with free will to make choices, while ultimately being held accountable before God for their choices.

Understanding this, Christians can expect opposition, criticism and labelling as bigots for not joining hands with secular society's modern definition of religious tolerance.

But, after all, is not Christianity the story of the One who laid down His life for the salvation of the world, and paid the supreme price for doing so? Submitting to the will of God as Jesus did is always the self- sacrificing mandate of Christian baptism and discipleship!

drsteadmore@starmail.com

Chapter Eighteen

BARCLAY always looked forward to his weekly coffee gathering at the Bean Bar Coffee Shop with Fr. Joseph and Fr. David. It was Fr. David's turn to buy so Barclay and Fr. Joseph found a comfortable booth while Fr. David placed their orders.

Their conversations usually began with each other relating how the previous seven days had transpired and then progressed to some theological issue that had recently made the news. It was amazing how the three always seemed to end up on the same page over each controversial subject that had made the media headlines.

"There is not much new under the sun, is there?" remarked Fr. Joseph. "It has been that way for decades. Declining attendance on Sunday morning, some scandal in the ranks of the clergy, a new law passed by the legislature limiting Christian symbols to be displayed in public buildings. Just recently, no public grants for summer student employment if an organization does not agree with abortion on demand. Don't you get the feeling we Christians are being attacked from all quarters?"

Before either Barclay or Fr. David could answer, a man approached their table and interrupted their conversation. He handed each a business card and continued on his way from table to table doing the same, never saying a word to anyone.

"What's this?" inquired Fr. David, as each began to examine the card in hand.

It read:

"THIS CARD IS FREE. IT IS WORTH NOTHING, BUT IT IS FREE!"

All three looked at one another and burst out laughing.

"This fellow must be a fan of Kris Kristofferson," quipped Barclay. "Do you remember his famous quote? 'Nothing ain't worth nothing, but it's free.'"

"Do you think that Kris Kristofferson intended the double negative … 'nothing' with 'ain't' … thereby making the claim that there must be something that is worth nothing?" queried Fr. David.

"That's the way I'd interpret him, fellows. Otherwise, I'm puzzled as to what he means. But as for this card we've been handed, I'm at a loss to make much out of it!" replied Fr. Joseph.

"Let's focus on your interpretation, David. Let's play with the idea that with Kristofferson's double negatives, that there must be things then in life that are worth nothing, but free, to which I disagree! Rather, I suggest that we reduce it all down to the expression: Nothing is free! What do you think we can do with that statement, fellows?"

"Flesh out a little more of what you mean, Steadmore. I'm listening."

"Well, I believe that the best things in life are not free," replied Barclay. "Everything that is worth something in life costs you something. If it doesn't cost you personally, it costs someone else. There is always a price attached to life's choices!

"Freedom certainly is not free! Terrible costs have been paid for it. And there is certainly a high cost to maintain freedom.

"Think of all the areas of life that we must work on to maintain them. Our marriages, our jobs, the raising of our children, our obligations as citizens in society, taxes, retirement preparations, the welfare of the disadvantaged. If a segment of society refuses to participate in making a fair share of a benevolent and caring society, then the costs increase for those who are left to pay the price for all to share!"

"Even death is not free, is it Steadmore?" replied Fr. Joseph. "No one dies without someone in life feeling the cost … a spouse, a child, grandchildren, relatives. Separation is emotionally costly. The simplest funeral is expensive!"

"Don't forget the great cost of death for the one who dies if the person has not lived a dedicated, committed life walking with Jesus Christ. Judgment is God's of course, but the Holy Scriptures call upon each individual to live out the demands of one's baptism. It is all too common to go through life shirking one's religious duties!" added Fr. David. "It is the price we Christians are obligated to pay. For Jesus said in Luke 9:23 'If any want to become my followers, let them deny themselves and take up their cross daily and follow me.' . Don't you believe in God's grace, David? Won't God's grace be sufficient to cover a person's multitude of sins?"

"Grace is indeed God's free gift Steadmore. But grace can be rejected, can't it? Even accepting God's grace requires our participation!" came back Fr. David. "You know that! The cost of grace was the life of Christ on the cross."

"We're all sitting here this morning breathing air and drinking a drink made with water," smiled Fr. Joseph. "And even the air and the water are not free. We're now in an age where both need protection

... at a cost to our wallets. Those costs are about to get even more expensive, especially if we delay in addressing the problem."

"Don't forget the cost to society if we clergy and the laity don't do everything in our power to propagate the Christian faith. Secular society is obsessed with trying to silence the influence of the Church. Without the message of Christ proclaimed in the social order, it is a downhill journey for hope without divine authority in a decadent, anything goes, secular community," summed up Barclay.

"Time's up guys," remarked Fr. David, as he stuffed that puzzling business card in his shirt pocket. "I've got to go! That was really a good time together this morning! Here's a challenge... come back next week with a topic to discuss. Let's see who can introduce a complex issue worthy of our theological expertise. Oh, and by the way ... you two received something for nothing this morning. Remember, it was I who picked up the tab!"

Chapter Nineteen

BARCLAY was in his study. It was 10:42 a.m. and he was struggling to come up with a topic for his next submission for the *Tangleville Mirror*. The coffee to the right of his Mac was growing cold. Perhaps he had best shut down the computer and go for a walk in the park. Maybe the muse would hit him, as it often had done in the past when he least expected it. Sometimes one can't force the mind to incite inspired thoughts!

"Barclay, you have received a rather large package in the mail from the *Tangleville Mirror*," Faith shouted from the kitchen. "Do you want it now, or later?"

"It couldn't have arrived at a better time, Faith! I'm at a dry spot with my creative juices. Do you mind handing me the package? I think I know what is in it."

Barclay tore open the package and it turned out that he was right about the contents.

During that last meeting with James Parker and Samantha Birkley in Parker's office, he had requested that he be forwarded samples of letters to the editor that followed some of his submissions for publication. He wanted, in particular, to discover how the readership was receiving his columns. He wanted to know the sentiments expressed by those who agreed and those who objected to the positions he took in his editorials. Would the subtitle that he always used at the beginning of each submission, the phrase "Does Father Know Best?" cause people to react positively or negatively to his theological positions often apparent in his writings. He was about to find out as he began to wade through selected letters to the editor found in the package.

The one on top of the pile was attached with a yellow sticker and the words of James Parker:

"Dr.—this is as good as it gets for stirring up controversy in our readership. Well done!"

The first letter to the editor didn't address any one particular submission that Barclay had written. Rather, it was so hostile that it must have divided Tangleville's readership!

WHO DOES HE THINK HE IS?

> I have never written a letter to an editor before, but I can't take it any longer! That priest Steadmore upsets me so badly that I cannot function for half a day every time I read one of his submissions.

> No! Father does not know best! First of all, he isn't my father! To me, a free thinker, his religious overtones in most of his articles are totally in opposition to the progressive movements of our age. His submissions are nothing more than sermons to the out-of-date Sunday church attenders.

Our enlightened age has long ago moved from being brow beaten and held hostage to religion, especially Christianity! No one can prove to me that God exists, and until someone does, I remain totally free from religious constraints. I am the master of my own destiny! No one who wears the religious title "Father" speaks for me! Do yourself and your readership a favour and fire Steadmore from your editorial staff!

Sincerely,

Clara Lipp, Tangleville

Barclay was divided over the article. James Parker was obviously pleased with this letter, but he himself felt that Ms. Lipp had completely missed the point of his submissions.

Yes! His submissions certainly were biased towards a Christian perspective, but she, being so anti-church, clearly felt that he was trying to coerce her into becoming more of a spiritual individual. Parker wanted to sell newspapers, but his aim was to present ideas to people who might reconsider long-held views on what makes for a better society in which to live.

The word "progressive" certainly had some merit, but change for the sake of change, especially if long-held religious standards are being dismissed, is not something to be lightly cast aside. To many in our age, progressive change often means that what was long held as religious based conduct can be discarded, and secular morality devoid of biblical principles surfaces ... conduct devoid of traditional spiritual based standards.

"I wonder," thought Barclay, "if I am only fooling myself. Maybe Parker wants my submissions only because he has increased readership in mind, and he is simply using me as a means to do so?"

Barclay quickly glanced through the letters to the editor, keeping a tab on how many seemed to convey appreciation for his submissions, and how many took opposition to his articles.

The following letter boosted his resolve to keep on sending material for publication, at least for the near future:

I NEVER PROMISED YOU A ROSE GARDEN

I read with appreciation Dr. Steadmore's recent article addressing the topic of unwanted, difficult, and stressful events in life. He handled well the answer to those who ask that if God is in control, why does He permit pain, suffering, accidents, and evil to exist?

Quoting from Lynn Anderson's 1970 hit song "Rose Garden" really was an excellent means to address a theological answer to long held views that God is not fair in allowing such unwanted conditions for the human race.

When I read the expression by Steadmore that perhaps "God has his reasons," I had to rethink long-held personal answers as to why events in my own life took place, finally admitting that my ways are not God's ways. I was finally able to accept the words of St. Paul in Romans 8:28, where he wrote, "We know that all things work together for good for those who love God, who are called according to His purpose."

It certainly is true that God never promised a "rose garden" in which to reside in this life, but He did promise that those who walk by faith, hand-in-hand with Jesus Christ, will be able to traverse the thorns, which spring up along the journey.

Where faith exists, grace triumphs!
Julia LaJoy, Tangleville

"Well, that woman got it," mused Barclay.

He was feeling more and more assured of the value of composing submissions for future articles. After he finished reading the twenty-two letters in Parker's mailing, the final tally was a ratio of two-to-one in appreciation of his opinions expressed versus those offended.

"That's OK," concluded Barclay. "I'll let Parker be pleased with those who rile up his readership. Maybe a win-win situation for the both of us is at work."

Barclay had promised that he would return all letters to the editor which had been forwarded to him. He wrote a thank-you note to James, placed it in an envelope, and walked out to the kitchen to join Faith.

"Let's go for a walk down to the Sip and Savour Bake Shop. We haven't done so in a couple of weeks. What do you say?"

"Give me five minutes to take a blueberry pie out of the oven. Can you wait that long?"

"For a blueberry pie, I'd walk to the coffee shop alone, bring you back a coffee and a critter and hurry back with them for you. But, I'll gladly wait five minutes!"

Faith smiled to herself. Barclay was as easy to read as a traffic sign!

Chapter Twenty

THE short walk to their favourite bake shop was always such an enjoyable time out of the day. The three blocks from their condo gave them time to wave to a few passing vehicles. Drivers usually honked their horns when they recognized the two walking hand in hand. Trinity Harbour was just big enough to provide all the amenities of modern living, yet small enough in which to make friends. Many in town were readers of the *Tangleville Mirror* sent to them from friends and relatives in the much larger community.

Barclay and Faith walked to the coffee counter and ordered their regular sized cups. Faith then found a table for two while Barclay proceeded to the baked goods section and purchased an apple critter and a lemon cruller. He had just rejoined Faith when Carrie Spencer approached their table. She was on for another conversation.

"Dr. Steadmore, I'm so glad to see you again." Not even glancing over to acknowledge the presence of Faith, she continued.

"I'm such a big huge fan of yours! Remember we met a few weeks ago here in this shop, and I asked you at that time if you would write an article which I could submit to my Pastor over at the Open Bible Fundamentalist Church? Remember, I said that he claims his congregation belongs to the only true denomination in Christendom. My daughter lives in Tangleville and sends me all the articles which you write for the paper. As I told you the last time, I don't have enough knowledge of church history to personally challenge him."

Faith was smiling as she looked straight at Barclay giving him a knowing wink. Over the years, she had become accustomed to female fans cornering her husband with all sorts of personal requests. She was well aware that male clergy become idolized as professionals who are good listeners, sympathetic to the needs of individuals who have few in life to approach for attention.

Clergy, especially male clergy, are considered as being safe to confide one's inner perceived requirements, especially when the troubled seeker has no one else to turn to. Clergy are not expected to charge a fee for giving advice.

Faith, once again, was willing to remain in her seat, pretend she wasn't there, and let yet another admirer of her husband have her audience recognized.

It was always interesting to sit back and wonder how her mate was going to handle requests, especially this one of Carrie's.

Barclay, speaking directly to his trusting admirer, not inviting her to sit down for a long chat, and in a low voice so others around would have difficulty hearing what he was about to say, began: "Carrie, you are asking something of me that I have no right to pursue. Your pastor is a trained theologian. He is more than qualified to promote the theology of his denomination. You, on the other hand, need to do research on the history of the Christian church, beginning with the early church Fathers, the many historic councils of bishops, the theology behind the creeds, and discover why so many denominations now exist. Some historians claim that Christendom now is so divided that over 33,000 separate competing denominations strive for adherents. It is the scandal of Christendom that we can't agree on what our Lord taught, that we all may be one in the faith.

"Your pastor's denomination then is one of thirty-thousand-plus varieties of Christianity. What do you think are the chances, the likelihood of his denomination being the one that is absolutely pure and authentic?

"It is you, Carrie, that must decide where you fit into the present smorgasbord of denominations. It is not your role to challenge your pastor's theological foundation for ministry. If you decide, after doing some serious research on the Church, that your present denomination is lacking, then find a denomination that you consider is more theologically historic and seek membership. It is you, Carrie, not your pastor, that needs to change!"

Barclay waited for Carrie's response. Faith remained silent and continued to munch away at her cruller.

"Dr. Steadmore, where can I get such reading materials that you suggest I read?"

"Go online and research texts and books for beginning the study of Church history. Then order personal copies at your downtown bookstore. You'll be a new person in your understanding of the development of Christianity if you do so.

"Good luck. Faith and I have an appointment to keep."

Carrie thanked Barclay, and as she turned to proceed back to her table, Faith whispered to Barclay: "What is the appointment you just told her you have to keep?"

"It is one with Faith Steadmore," grinned her husband. "Now let's keep our date with each other!"

Barclay and Faith walked hand in hand back to their condo. There was no need for conversation. Each, after years of marriage, could read each other like a cherished verse of Scripture.

Except for Carrie Spencer's intrusion, it had been a perfect date.

Chapter Twenty-One

OF the many submissions Barclay had forwarded to the *Tangleville Mirror*, one topic he had up to now not addressed was growing more urgent in his thinking: Does life have a purpose? If so, what is it? Can humanity know for certain the answer to these ancient questions?

Barclay decided that he needed to attempt to come to grips with such questions, knowing full well that some of his readership was bound to disagree with his conclusions ... even to angrily disagree.

It was early on the next Tuesday morning following his and Faith's encounter with Carrie Spencer's episode at the Sip and Savour Bake Shop that he sat down at his desk, before his Mac, and began to type.

WHAT IS THE PURPOSE OF LIFE?

Does Father Know Best?

by The Rev. Canon Dr. Barclay Steadmore

Have you ever pondered the following questions? What is the purpose of life? What are the intentions of your life? Does your answer matter? Are you willing to re-evaluate your present conclusions?

Over the centuries, the greatest minds have wrestled with these most perplexing philosophical questions.

Some have attempted to rewrite the challenge by asking another question: What is it that makes life worth living?

Answers to this rephrased way of avoiding the array of the deeper questions above are much simpler and easier to address.

Epicurus, the Greek philosopher (341-270 BCE), stated: "Pleasure is the first good. It is to be the beginning of every choice and every aversion. It is the absence of pain in the body and troubles of the soul."

Commonly paraphrased as "the most amount of pleasure with the least amount of pain" down through the ages, this ideal has become the popular answer for the purpose of life.

As rational beings, it is acknowledged that not one of us asks to be born, and very few seek means to die (suicide and assisted euthanasia excepted). All humans know that eventually death waits, regardless of how one may take every effort to prolong life: the proper diet, physical exercise, avoidance of unhealthy lifestyles, a positive mental attitude, vitamin supplements, and so forth. But death waits, regardless!

Knowing this, another question needs to be addressed. Do we simply live for ourselves, or does our existence affect others around us? Striving to make the world around us a better place to live, seeking justice, equality, fair play, pursuing knowledge for scientific discoveries, eradication of disease, poverty, hunger, the establishment of peace—all of these pursuits are admirable, laudable and have merit. Robert F. Kennedy summed it up when he said, "The purpose of life is to contribute in some way to making things better." But such pursuits do not eliminate eventual, individual death.

Consequently one, if one is perfectly honest, is eventually forced to ask the inevitable question: Is life a joke?

Perhaps, Johann Wolfgang von Goethe, in *The Sorrows of Young Werther,* put it perfectly when he said, "The human race is a monotonous affair. Most people spend the greatest part of their time working in order to live, and what little freedom remains so fills them with fear that they seek out any and every means to be rid of it."

If nothing is absolute, but life itself only has value to the self or to others, how do we get a consensus on the best or the worst? Is the joke on humanity?

Those who believe in the existence of a supreme Creator, God will emphatically say, "No! Life is not a joke!" For if God exists, then the concept of life is expanded: physical life between one's birth and one's eventual last breath, followed by eternal life-spiritual existence.

For Christians (and the other faiths which believe in life after death), then the final days of one's physical existence are time to prepare for one's resurrected state of being.

Consequently, instead of filling one's earthly days attempting to seek "the greatest amount of pleasure, with the least amount of pain," instead of making secular work or the pursuit of some chosen task a priority, those who follow God's will believe that the purpose of life revolves around doing God's will. The prophet Micah clarifies the purpose of human existence: "He has told you, O mortal what is good; and what does the Lord require of you, but to do justice, and love kindness, and walk humbly with your God" (Micah 6:8).

Matthew 22:37-39 gave his listeners the following commandment: "You shall love the Lord your God with all your heart, and with all your soul, and with all your mind. This is the greatest and the first commandment. And the second is like it: You shall love your neighbour as yourself."

Consequently, the purpose of life for Christians is to please God and to be His agents who participate in the coming of the Kingdom of Heaven.

For non-believers in a Supreme God, the judge of all, the consequences of not seeking His purpose in life is no "joke." Galatians 6:7 is very clear: "Do not be deceived. God will not be mocked, for you reap whatever you sow."

Have you still not come to grips with my original four questions posed at the beginning of this article? You have no choice but to decide your answers, for if God exists, the purpose of life is already determined.

Note: The atheist will challenge this last statement and will say, "Prove to me that God exists, for if He doesn't, the joke is on those who gave their lives over to pursuing Biblical principles." My answer to the atheist is, "Prove to me that

God doesn't exist." Then, follow up with the statement, "That makes you and me gamblers, doesn't it?" As for me, I'm betting my life on the fact that He does exist and that venture then defines the absolute purpose of my being.

drsteadmore@starmail.com

Barclay closed down his Mac, stretched, and called out to Faith. "Want to go for a drive? It is a beautiful day. We can put the top down and take a drive out into the county."

"Give me five minutes," replied Faith. "I'll do the driving!"

Chapter Twenty-Two

AT the close of last Friday's coffee gathering, now a weekly event, the three clerics had departed agreeing to give some thought to what each considered to be the most complex theological and politically diverse issue in our modern age. Barclay had been wrestling with this matter for some time.

He finally settled on a most divisive issue, one that he considered most modern Christians to be facing: Abortion on demand. Even though the Holy Scriptures are silent on the topic, Christianity is facing hostile criticism for speaking out on the sanctity of human life, as some put it, from "womb to tomb."

Certainly, the two most opposing views on abortion center around the right of an expectant mother to choose whether or not to bring the fetus to a natural birth, versus the right of a fetus to be protected until viability. A mother's right to autonomy of her body over the right of the developing human being for full protection until birth. Secular society, the medical profession, legal experts, even Christendom is divided on the topic.

Barclay was looking forward to Fr. David's and Fr. Joseph's choices to begin their Friday discussion. On the following Wednesday, Barclay had sent an e-mail to remind each to be prepared to discuss their answer to the assignment.

When Friday rolled around, Barclay was pulling into the parking lot at the same time that Fr. Joseph was arriving in his SUV.

"Still driving that Lexus? After winning that $2,000,000? I expected you to arrive in a Bentley," teased Barclay.

Fr. Joseph smiled from ear to ear. "I'll fill you in over coffee when Fr. David arrives. Can't wait to bring you up to date on the lottery win."

Fr. David arrived five minutes after the two clerics had already chosen a booth as far away from the morning crowd as possible. They knew that listening ears would likely be tuned in when their conversation got under way.

"Hey, David," Joseph greeted the tardy cleric. "It's your turn to buy the coffee this morning. I'll have a large coffee, double cream, and a cheese croissant. What about you Barclay?"

"Make it a large double cream and a blueberry critter."

Fr. David returned with a tray loaded for what was likely to be a lengthy discussion time together. "Steadmore, it is your turn next week!" grinned Fr. David. " I can hardly wait to order up with you picking up the tab!"

It was, as usual, to be another of the most looked forward to times of the week for each of the three. They, in spite of their different theological backgrounds, had become great friends and valued each other's commitment to live out the mandate of their ordination vows.

"OK, Father," began Dr. David. "What did you decide to do with that windfall of yours? Do you still feel comfortable associating with us two financially struggling retired ecclesiastics?"

"I'm back with you two frugal men of the cloth fellows. I can't wait to tell you why."

Fr. Joseph was bubbling over with excitement as he outlined how he, with the help of his lawyer, had set up a trust fund for assisting new immigrants, single parents, laid off workers, and various other needy people, where all requests would be evaluated by a small Board of Directors, five in number, with Fr. Joseph as the Chair. Requests for donations to worthy causes would be considered from time to time.

"The $2,000,000 was entrusted to a well-known investment firm, where each year, the interest gained could be dispersed to those who required help ... individuals and groups would be required to submit applications for consideration by the Board.

"It's set up, fellows, so that the trust fund will exist for perpetuity ... the lottery people who turned the cheque over to me and took my photo were not very impressed when I told them that I hadn't purchased the winning ticket, that it was gift, and I didn't personally believe in gambling. But they tried to put the best spin on the event to make it appear that the public could be as lucky as me.

"So you see fellows, I'm back to being as financially limited as you guys!"

Their conversation eventually got around to Barclay's e-mail, which reminded them that they were to come today with what each felt was the greatest challenge for Christian intervention in the modern secular age.

Since Barclay had sent the e-mail, he assumed the role of the chairperson. "Who's going to go first, fellows?"

Fr. Joseph was quick to respond. "Abortion and fetal rights.

"I agree," spoke up Fr. David. "I thank God that my mother believed in pro-life. I certainly can't believe in abortion serving as a means of contraception. At first, I couldn't decide between abortion on demand and assisted suicide. But since the abortion procedure is now so common, and far outnumbers the second one, I go with that being the greatest challenge for Christian intervention. Both are repugnant, but frequency of occurrence dictates my answer."

"So Steadmore, what is your answer?" requested Fr. Joseph.

"Well gentlemen, it is unanimous. I totally agree. It must be the Holy Spirit working. So what do we propose, as retired clerics, to do about it?"

Barclay continued. "I've always been troubled by how final an abortion is. One can have an abortion and repent the deed, but one cannot reverse the results of the procedure … the act itself. One never gets the opportunity to restore the life of the innocent victim."

"Steadmore, you are talking with retired clergy. We're all out of the pulpit, so to speak. People are not willing to listen to such politically incorrect voices such as ours," countered Fr. David. "Secular society has tuned us out and banished us to the annals of ancient history! Secularists will never listen to our voices."

"Besides, Steadmore," protested Fr. Joseph, "My denomination is already protesting the evils of abortion by lining the sidewalks with parishioners carrying anti-abortion plaque cards. This approach simply allows the pro-choice passers-by to give the finger to well-meaning pro-lifers … or a shouted out insult through the vehicle's open window. It doesn't work! Such well-intentioned objectors simply empower the pro-choice advocates!"

"But what if there is a better way to engage and counter such vocal protestors … where no one is present to hear them … where shouting would fall on absolutely deaf ears?" grinned Steadmore.

"If you are suggesting that we send letters to the editor of our local paper, signed by the three of us, outlining our objections to the evils of abortion, forget it Steadmore! It will only encourage and enable the secular crowd to write their letters countering ours. I don't want to give them another avenue to voice their objections."

"I'm with you fellows. The last thing we want to do is give the pro-choice group the opportunity to stage a photo-op where they outshout the opposing voices. But what if there are no voices to outshout?"

"OK, Steadmore, we know that you are about to spring something on us. Let's have it!"

Barclay was more than ready. "Concentrate on that fast food restaurant chain that under it's big capital letter logo, that sign you can see from blocks away, that informs customers of the ever-growing number of how many have been served around the world. The restaurant chain has stopped changing the number, and now simply says 'billions served.' I don't know about you, but I liked it better when the sign indicated positive growth. It was a curiosity element at work, I guess. I loved it! It was a silent, no shouting, informative bragging device that worked so effectively."

"Where are you going with this?" interrupted Fr. David.

Barclay could hardly contain his enthusiasm. "I'm proposing that we invent a portable, highly visible, electronic sign … perhaps one that could fit in the bed of a pickup truck, or on its own trailer wheels … perhaps a sign in the design and form of a big capital 'A.' I'm talking about an abortion clock, with live digital numbers within the frame that are constantly changing … informing onlookers of actual minute-to-minute abortions taking place.

"The sign would not exhibit any audible noise. It would be simply silent! Informative! Protesters would not be able to shut it down. It would be immune to passers-by, but always changing the up-to-the-minute statistical information. The curiosity element would be so powerful, that even those who are adamantly pro-choice would find it almost impossible not to glance at when they are passing by it."

"I need more detail, Barclay," queried Fr. Joseph. "What kind of information would the clock display?"

"It would be programmed to change its readout every ten minutes or so, for example reading, 'The number of abortions today in Canada,' next perhaps in the US … in the world to date. The numbers would be live … constantly adding up … the frequency of the changing digits being the reminder that at the very moment in time, abortions are taking place. I think that there are thousands of people in the world who are totally unaware of the frequency of the procedure … out of sight, out of mind, so to speak, the data that pro-choice people want to be hidden from society. If the general public was to be made aware of how common abortion is in our age, there would, I believe, be a cry of outrage and protest."

"How would such a device be powered?" piped up Fr. David, the ever-practical one of the three. "By solar energy, David. The device would contain its own built-in photo electric cells and battery storage so that it wouldn't need to be plugged in anywhere it may be parked."

"Would it need a permit to be parked on display property?"

"No, since it wouldn't be displayed on town or city land, but most likely on church properties, usually temporary locations, and then not becoming a fixed sign. When it is carried about on wheels behind a pickup truck, it of course would be mobile and no permit needed."

"I like the idea Barclay," responded Fr. Joseph. "But this is a new device not yet in existence. How do you propose that we get it or build it? We would need engineers, welders, electronic experts, research people to keep tabs on the daily data to program into the device, maybe even web designers to keep it functioning. And besides all this, how much would it cost? Can we afford such an undertaking?"

"Ah," came back Barclay. "We will also want to patent the device, insure it, and devise ways to protect it against vandalism. But it can be done. With the vast resources of the churches and the pro-life movement in society, I'm certain that there will be willing and ready volunteers, experts, professionals, who will come onside and provide the expertise to design it and to fund it. It must be a non-denominational undertaking, not promoting or sponsored by any one Christian denomination, but available to all who wish to use it. I already think that I know a devout Christian, a Greek orthodox, who would be willing to put substantial funds into its creation."

The conversation between the three priests extended far longer than the usual time they spent during a regular Friday coffee meeting. The meeting finally ended with all three agreeing that they were onboard, provided that the monies could be raised to design the device, and that professional experts could be found in local parishes to contribute to its conception.

"All right, fellows," summed up Barclay. "Let's agree that we will go to work during the next few days, come up with names of those parishioners who have the capabilities, competence, and potential interest in such a project, and meet as usual next Friday morning. What do you say?"

"Agreed!" David and Joseph chimed in together.

"I think that I already know an organization that controls a trust fund that may be willing to advance some money for the project. I'll speak to the chairperson," grinned Fr. Joseph.

"Now who in the world could that person be?" piped up Fr. David as he gave Fr. Joseph a playful nudge to the left shoulder.

Barclay could hardly wait to get home to give a call to Annie Sting.

Chapter Twenty-Three

AS Barclay was on his way back to the condo, the light on the dash of the Mustang illuminated, indicating that the convertible was low on fuel. "Better fill it up or Faith won't have enough gas to do her weekly grocery shopping this afternoon," he thought to himself.

As he was filling up at the self-serve filling station, a green minivan pulled into the space on the opposite side of his pump. The back window was down and a cute blonde-haired girl, about four or five years of age, shouted over to him.

"Hey mister! Do you want to see my new music box? Mummy just bought it for me. You have to wind it up to play a tune."

"Sure!" replied Barclay. After checking with the girl's mother who was already pumping gas if it was all right to do so, Barclay reached over, gently accepted the brightly decorated box, which was about five inches side to side, and replied, "This is so pretty. What am I supposed to do?"

"Wind it up with that little crank on the side?"

Barclay proceeded to wind the crank clockwise and the box began to play an old time nursery rhyme tune:

I'm a little teapot, short and stout,

Here is my handle, here is my spout.

When I get all steamed up, hear me shout,

Tip me over and pour me out!

"Can we sing it together?" Barclay invited the little girl. They did, and when the tune was finished, they smiled at each other.

"Now mister, wind the crank in the opposite direction!"

Barclay had hardly made five turns of the crank when the lid flew open and a jack-in-the-box popped out, almost hitting him in the nose.

The little girl laughed hysterically.

"I love your music box, little girl. What is your name?"

"Faith."

"That is also my wife's name. It is a word straight out of the Bible. Do you go to Sunday School?"

"What is Sunday School, mister?"

The girl's mother was ready to drive off, so Faith and Barclay said "goodbye." He finished pumping his gas, and having paid at the pump, he continued on his journey home.

"What was that all about?" he thought to himself. "There must be a theological message somewhere behind that little delightful incident."

"What's Sunday School, mister?" he repeated to himself.

"The question was not so unexpected in this age," he thought. "More and more people in secular society have dismissed religion from their daily lives. The little girl was simply an archetype of our time," he concluded. "No need for God when everything is going well and modern society has intervened in the once relied upon social outreach of organized religion. At one time religious denominations established hospitals, schools, welfare assistance for the homeless … now governments head up and provide."

Driving home it occurred to Barclay that the counter-clockwise cranking of the music box releasing the jack-in-the-box was also thought provoking ... maybe even an indication of how it takes an unexpected event to jar one into thinking, as they say, "out of the box!"

When he had cranked the box in the normal direction, he triggered the expected music of the nursery rhyme. But when he reversed the procedure, a totally different effect transpired.

"Isn't that the way it is with the message of Christianity today," he mused. "People know about the basic tenants of Christianity, but simply anticipate the mundane, the old-fashioned message to be expected when the topic is discussed. How many people, in this secular age, really are caught up in nursery rhymes when electronic play stations and modern electronic games are all the rage?"

It was the surprise element of the box that intrigued the little girl. And so it is, perhaps with how the church ought to present its message in a fashion that surprises ... even annoys the blasé recipient.

"That is exactly what our Abortion Clock is likely to do with those who encounter it," he smiled to himself. "Either to be confronted with facts that may make the complacent viewer rethink one's attitude toward the subject, or be so annoyed that one may want to shut it down. Either way, the Church will have accomplished its mission ... to bring the procedure of abortion as a common means of birth control back into the parlours of a jaded society.

"I think that the three of us may be up to something that may startle the contemporary masses. Can't wait to make a phone call!"

Upon arriving at his condo, Barclay proceeded to his study, picked up the phone, and dialed the Sting residence in Tangleville.

"Hello, Annie speaking."

"Annie, it's Barclay calling. Am I interrupting anything? Shall I call back later?"

"No, no! Great timing! I've just got in from an appointment with my hair stylist downtown. I feel like a new woman," laughing as she said it.

"Annie, is Harry around? I don't want to speak to him, this call is between you and me."

" No. Harry is at an in-camera council meeting at the city hall. He won't be back until late this afternoon."

"Annie, great! I've got to bend your ear for a few minutes. There are two topics I need to discuss with you."

Barclay proceeded to tell her how he and two friends of his, Fr. Joseph and Fr. David, have been meeting every Friday morning for the past few months. He talked about how they, being retired, spend their time together discussing the needs and problems of contemporary society. Barclay, with great enthusiasm, outlined their plans to design and implement an Abortion Clock to silently inform a complacent secular public of the numerical facts of the procedure.

"Annie, here is a start-up hurdle that needs to first be addressed: funds for its design and construction. Now Annie, I want your honest and open opinion. Can you sympathize with what we are up to? Are you with us in attempting to counter the pro-abortion movement in our modern worldly society?"

"Absolutely, Barclay! You know that I am an Orthodox Christian. Of course I strongly disapprove of abortion when it is used solely as a means of birth control."

"Annie, Fr. David is an Orthodox Priest. I knew how you were likely to answer, but I wanted to get your personal answer. Is there any possibility that you might advance some funds for us to get started on our rather radical effort to confront the issue?"

"Absolutely, Canon! I'll make out a cheque to you as soon as we hang up. How's a gift, not a loan, of $20,000? What is your second topic?"

"Annie, I'm speechless! A million thank-yous!

"But, before you decide to drop the cheque in the mail, there is one more thing I need to tell you. It is very likely that when the device is built and operational, it may first be on display in Tangleville. Now it will certainly be a divisive event. Sooner or later, Harry is going to be confronted for his opinion on the matter, and sooner or later the press will discover that you, his spouse, helped finance the undertaking. This may divide his voting support in his ward in the coming election for council members. Do you think that Harry may want to take the risk of losing his seat for such a religious-based principle?"

"I already know what he will say to me when I tell him of your concern. But I'll speak to him before I mail the cheque. He's a man of principle who will put his faith convictions before secular ambition. I'll e-mail you after I talk with him. Expect my cheque in a few days!"

"Bless you Annie! Faith doesn't know that I am calling you, but if she had known, she would have sent her love."

"It looks like this endeavour may get off the ground," Barclay smiled to himself. "I can hardly wait for next Friday to inform Joseph and David. God certainly works in mysterious ways! They may be as surprised as I was when that jack-in-the-box flew up and nearly struck me in the nose."

Chapter Twenty-Four

BARCLAY had been putting off writing an article about an idea that had been fermenting in his mind for some time: The role of religious faith in the practice of modern medicine. He was aware that he was not a graduate of medical school or a registered clinical psychologist, but, as a priest, he had witnessed the healing power of prayer and faith countless times in his parish ministry, both in hospital settings and as a result of counselling sessions. It was time to put pen to paper to address the topics and then to forward the article to the *Tangleville Mirror*.

IF THE CHURCH IS A HOSPITAL, WHAT IS THE MEDICINE?

Does Father Know Best?

by The Rev. Canon Dr. Barclay Steadmore

From the time of the birth of Christianity and throughout the early centuries, the Church was the hospital for its adherents. Faith and healing were integrated. The Epistle of St. James states:

"Are any among you suffering? They should pray … And are any among you sick? They should call for the elders of the Church and have them pray over them, anointing them with oil in the name of the Lord. The prayer of faith will save the sick and the Lord will raise them up; and anyone who has committed sins will be forgiven" (James 5:13-15).

As knowledge developed, with science dealing with that which is subject to physical measurements, experimentations, chemical and surgical treatments, the spiritual aspect of life in the healing modus was gradually rejected. Now in our modern age, medical science limits itself to that which is physical, observable, and repeatable. Consequently, the modern concept of the person has splintered when the diseases of the physical body are concerns of medical doctors, problems of the mind are in the realms of psychology and psychiatry, which also involves prescription medicine, and spiritual matters are left to priests and pastors to address.

Now when the word "hospital" is used, one naturally thinks of a building ... bricks and mortar, filled with modern medical inventions, x-ray machines, MRIs, CT scans, operating rooms, and recovery beds.

But in more recent times, in medical science, we find a growing body of scientific evidence that the medical treatment of the body alone is lacking in the overall treatment and wellness recovery of the sick. Medical science by itself falls short in its treatment of our thoughts, feelings, and emotions, which each, and or all, play a role in controlling many physiological processes.

Addiction, hypertension, chronic inflammatory syndromes, guilt, and so forth can affect the immune system. The doors open to treatment of such conditions lie once again with spirituality, where faith, prayer and participation in religious activities and the sacrificial rites of the Church have a positive effect on health and recovery beyond conventional medical procedures. Consequently, the Church is now, once again, a hospital for the cure of the soul: mind, body, and spirit ... for the health of the whole person. As Psalm 103:2-3 states: "Bless the Lord, O my soul, and do not forget his benefits—who forgives all your iniquities, who heals all your diseases."

Now the question is again relevant: "If the Church is a hospital, what is the medicine?"

In the healing process of the whole person, there is a growing body of scientific evidence that feelings and emotions, thoughts, stress, despair, rejection, sorrow, anguish, bitterness, even joy, are psychological conditions that are really spiritually related. Participation in prayer and the sacramental life of religious practitioners have a positive effect on health and recovery.

It must be noted that psychology and traditional medicinal procedures cannot forgive sin, absolve guilt, or heal a despairing heart. These are matters of the faith, the Holy Spirit, the intervention of God in one's life. Modern science now admits that a restored heart can, and does, strengthen the body.

The medicines, so to speak, are different but both are required. Physical technology of modern medicine is a true gift from God, but, is not the entire answer to the healing act. The Church as a hospital administers medicine of the spiritual nature. Conventional medicine and spiritual medicine are hand in glove as God's intervention in the maintenance of the "whole person."

Where appointments for consultations with doctors and specialists are limited to restricted intervals, the medical expert does not have the time to spend at length in listening or discussion. The priest or pastor does!

A clergyperson is a listener ... one who, like Jesus, conveys to the seeker the assurance that one is loved, accepted, worthy of one's presence and of God's acceptance. Medicine is not just an art to be applied to the infirmed, it's a spiritual practice! The latter is the domain of the Christian healer! Science can cure, but love, confession, forgiveness, trust, and faith heals! I close by expanding on the words of St. James:

Are any among you suffering ... are any among you sick? They should call for an appointment with the doctor and with the clergyperson. Each will lay hands upon you in vastly different fashions. The doctor may write a prescription ... the priest will pray over you, anoint you with holy oil blessed by the bishop, and will sign you with the sign of the cross, and the Lord will raise them up.

drsteadmore@starmail.com

Barclay shut down his Mac and turned to check the messages on his iPhone.

"Barclay, call me!" It was Harry's cell number.

Chapter Twenty-Five

IT sounded urgent! Barclay dialed Harry's cell number.

"Harry speaking!"

"Hi Harry. Got your message. Sorry to take so long in getting back to you. My phone was downstairs and I didn't hear it ring."

"No problem, my friend. But I'm glad you reached me. Do you have a few minutes? I need to talk!"

"I just finished an article for the *Tangleville Mirror*. I've got lots of time."

"Barclay, do you remember how we talked the last time we were together ... how I was concerned with possible conflicts of interest in my role as a town councillor, with my personal faith convictions? Well, I've run into one and I want your advice as how to handle it."

"Fill me in Harry!"

"When I ran for the position, I wasn't aware of the many social and political events, outside the council chambers, that one is expected to attend ... many of course in my own ward, but also during special events the town promotes. Some are a privilege to attend, indeed, even a joy to do so. Being there for Remembrance Day services, the Santa Claus parade, lunches and meetings with elected provincial and federal members …hosting visitors to town … they present no problem at all."

"But Harry, you didn't call me to tell me what you just outlined. What is it that really is troubling you?"

"Barclay, there are some public events that I can't justify supporting. My conscience gets in the way. My faith convictions won't allow it! And I've just received criticism in an article in the *Tangleville Mirror*. It is politically toxic. I didn't show up at last week's Gay Pride event along with the Mayor and the rest of the town councillors."

"Harry, let's start with you. Are you sorry that you made that decision not to attend?"

"No!"

"Would you trade your faith convictions for political gain?"

"No!"

"So what is the real concern for your call? It seems to me that you know who you are. Being true to yourself starts with knowing your strengths, passions, limitations, and purpose in life. You made a personal choice to demonstrate how you want to live and be understood as an elected representative of your ward."

"Barclay, I've upset a lot of people who don't share my faith convictions. I don't want to be a divisive disciple of Christ. I want to be seen as a person who unites … brings people together. It is going to happen again in the near future when Tangleville opens its first cannabis retail store, and I don't plan to attend the grand opening."

"Harry, listen! Being true to yourself means you don't worry about pleasing people, living by someone else's standards or rules. You have chosen as a baptized Christian to represent Christ in your daily walk of faith. Don't forget that our Lord was a divisive individual. He went to the cross without compromising His message.

"Being true to yourself is this simple … either you live in integrity as you interpret the Holy Scriptures, or you live 'out' of integrity. Compromise is not an option!"

"I know! I know! I guess that I just need to hear you say it."

"Harry, you haven't as much as said so, but are you worried about losing your seat in the next town election?"

"It has crossed my mind, Barclay."

"Are you willing to pay the price of sticking by your convictions, even if it costs you your town seat?"

"Yes, I am!"

"Then Harry, you have solved your non-existent moral predicament. You don't need me. But here is the good news! Your personal stance in not attending that parade may in fact win you a lot of votes from Christians in your ward. You may be seen as the someone whom they wish they could be … willing to walk the walk of faith. So many in today's world hold views and convictions that don't agree with secular society's 'anything goes' philosophy. Yet they won't say it, or openly oppose it. You, then, become their voices.

"I'm changing the topic: Harry, did Annie fill you in about our recent conversation regarding the plans to develop an Abortion Clock?"

"Yes, she did."

"And?"

"You've got my fullest support!"

"Harry, you may then soon be in the middle of another politically divisive event in a few months. If my two clergy friends and I get the clock off the drawing board, I'm going to push for it to be publicly launched in Tangleville. Is that OK with you?"

"You can count on it, Doctor. I'd gladly risk a few votes to put the issue before a complacent public! By the way, when are you and Faith coming back to Tangleville?"

"We think about it now and then Harry, but we are pretty comfortable here in Trinity Harbour. But who knows? We still find our hearts back with the many friends in your town. Keep in touch, Harry!"

Harry was not ready to say goodbye. The conversation continued for another ten minutes. Barclay could tell that Harry's voice indicated a heavy weight had been removed from his mind.

"Got to go, Harry! My regards to Annie. Tell her that she is a gem for her donation. You do know about it, don't you?"

"Annie does whatever she feels led to do. She is her own person!"

* * *

The week seemed to drag by. Barclay could hardly wait for Friday morning's meeting with Fr. David and Fr. Joseph.

Barclay was the first to arrive at the Bean Bar Coffee Shop. He was well aware of what his two friends would be ordering. They were so predictable!

Before the two clerics' arrival, Barclay had purchased the three cups of coffee and the dessert that he knew they would order. He picked up their treats, proceeded to find a table as far as possible from other customers in the shop, and sat down just as the two priests appeared.

"Doctor, you must be in a generous mood this morning," quipped Fr. David. "Did you win the lottery, or something?"

"Sit down fellows! Drink up and let's get down to business!"

"Well," interjected Fr. Joseph. "He must want to bring us some good news. I can hardly wait to let him bend our ears."

"Fellows, you may find this hard to believe, but we already have a $20,000 donation to begin our project. A friend of Faith's and mine, a Greek Orthodox Christian lady, is solidly behind the project. She lives in Tangleville and her husband, a member of the town council, are both excited to get things underway. How did you fellows make out?"

Fr. David was the first to respond. "God bless those Orthodox Christians! It doesn't surprise me a bit. But wait until I tell you some other welcome news. Two members of my former parish, both close friends, one an electrical engineer and the other with a Master's degree in computer science, each now retired, are willing to do the technical input for the project. They are only waiting for the financial means to begin. But, they advised me that they will need at least $30,000 to get underway."

"OK, Fr. Joseph," grinned Barclay, "What can the RCs do?"

"Way ahead of you guys! I spoke with the Board of Directors of my recently set up trust fund ... you know ... the one from the proceeds of my winning $2,000,000 lottery. With me chairing the board, and with my recommendation, the Board is willing to grant a long-term loan of $15,000 to get us off the ground. No interest involved, repayable over a twenty-year period. They think that our project is a great way to spend the lottery winnings."

"Wait until the lottery foundation hears that news," grinned Barclay. "That ought to put a different spin on their advertising to encourage buyers of tickets for personal gain, especially if the commission members lean towards pro-choice sentiments."

Barclay noticed that their coffee mugs were getting low. "We are going to need some more time to plan where we are to go from here. I'll get us another round of coffee!"

When he returned with fresh cups, Joseph and David were already sketching out details, on one of the coffee shop paper napkins, of the steps to proceed with design and production.

"Listen to this, Father. We suggest that we open a bank account with the $35,000 start-up funds … all three of us needed as co-signers on all issued cheques to get underway.

"We will let the two experts in David's old parish supply us with preliminary plans as to the site, design, and portability of the device. We can authorize them to get started right away, and report back to us in a week in time for next week's meeting. By then it will give us time to think about what we want the sign to display, a name for it, and how we are going to get the accurate up-to-date data for the machine to display. What do you think?"

"I say go for it! But one precautionary step needs to be taken. Not a word to anyone, especially to the media. If word leaks out, there will be an outcry of protest. We want the launch of the clock to be a total surprise … too late for objectors to attempt to stop the project. Agreed?"

"Of course, Barclay," responded Fr. David. "I'll authorize my two technical experts to get right on it."

They finished their second round of coffee, animated conversation demonstrating the excitement that the project was generating. It was obvious that the three retired clergy had found a renewed purpose in ministry … one that if materializing, had the potential to have far-reaching consequences in secular society. It was surely God the Holy Spirit working in a uniquely new twenty-first century fashion.

On the way home, Barclay's cell phone Bluetooth device kicked in. It was Faith calling.

"Bark, pick up a couple of rib eye steaks to barbecue for dinner. There is something waiting here for you when you arrive!"

Chapter Twenty-Six

BARCLAY dropped into the Gourmet Butcher Shop and selected two medium sized rib eyes. He was anxious to get home to find out what Faith meant when she told him that something was waiting for him. When he arrived, Faith was busy doing the week's laundry.

"Faith, your call has aroused my curiosity. What's up?"

"There is a large envelope on your desk addressed to you from the Office of the Bishop of New Avondale. We haven't kept in touch with the Diocese since moving to Trinity Harbour. Who is the present Bishop now that Bishop Strictman has been retired over a year?"

"I haven't met him yet! But, I have heard good things about him. His name is Bishop James Soulman. He's new to the Diocese."

"Well, you better open the letter, Bark. Maybe he wants you to come out of retirement and head up some project he has dreamed up. Ready to put the collar back on?" teased Faith.

Always the intuitive Faith, Barclay merely smiled, but didn't respond. He tore open the letter and proceeded to read it to Faith:

The Rev. Canon Dr. Barclay Steadmore
102 Contentment Dr., Unit 327
Trinity Harbour, Ontario M4D 5X2

Donald H. Hull

Dear Canon Dr. Barclay,

Greetings from the Diocese of New Avondale!

We have not personally met, but since I became Diocesan Bishop following the retirement of Bishop Strictman, I have heard on numerous occasions great things concerning your many years of leadership at St. Bartholomew's Parish. The parish is still growing and thriving. Well done, good and faithful servant!

Because of the continuing legacy of your skills in ministry, I would like you and your spouse, Faith, to give prayerful consideration to a one-year appointment, just newly opening up, with New Avondale's Companion Diocese of St. Paul's in Nigeria.

The position would be one that involves a number of duties: lecturing to clergy on various North American aspects of practical theology, how to deal with the secular media, inter-denominational Christian co-operation, and evangelism in the twenty-first century. From what I have learned of your long rectorship at St. Bart's and your media skills, I am convinced that you are the perfect candidate for the appointment.

Of course, financial means are available to assist you in the year-long appointment.

If you are interested, please make an appointment through my Administrative Archdeacon to meet with me in person. At such time, full details of the position will be discussed: airfare, personal transportation, housing, stipend, and free time for private travelling to neighbouring African countries.

I am most hopeful that you and Faith will respond positively to my proposal.

Sincerely,

+ James

The Rt. Rev. James Soulman,
Bishop, Diocese of New Avondale

Barclay folded the letter, placed it back in the envelope, and looked at Faith. "What do you make of that, Faith? I'm completely lost for words!"

"Well, I'm not surprised! For some time now, I've had the feeling that all your years of ministry were not going to end with retirement. It's only a year-long appointment. We both are enjoying good health. I say let's set up that appointment with Bishop Soulman and explore the request in a little more detail!"

"But Faith, what would we do with our condo for a year? And our Mustang? I'm right in the middle of those exciting plans with Fr. Joseph and Fr. David to go ahead with the building of the Abortion Clock. I don't want to drop that project. It's so revolutionary ... so timely in this secular age!"

"Now keep in mind that the Bishop didn't state a departure date for us. Maybe that is negotiable. The first thing to do is commit it all to prayer ... take it one step at a time."

"You're right, Faith. It is all so unexpected ... so different from what is expected of a normal retirement. At least, a meeting with the Bishop would give us both an excuse for a return trip to visit Tangleville.

"Want to put the top down and go for a coffee? I can't think right now about much else than that letter. A little wind in my hair is just what I need."

"Can't go just now Bark! I'm in the middle of baking for the coffee hour at the church following Sunday's 10:30 a.m. service. It is my turn to provide the muffins. Why don't you go for a ride by yourself?"

* * *

Barclay walked to the parking lot, lowered the top, put on his sunglasses and favourite driving cap and headed directly to the closest drive-thru coffee shop. With a medium dark roast, double cream, in the cup holder, he headed out of town to enjoy a drive through a paved, twisting country highway. The sun was shining, the temperature was in the high 20s and the Mustang and driver were in perfect sync.

Barclay's mind was in overdrive. What would Faith and he do with their condo during their twelve-month absence? And the Mustang? He couldn't bear to sell it! It would have to go into storage. There would be bills to pay monthly ... condo fees ... insurance ... town taxes and utility fees ... the list was long. Since he and Faith were not parents, they would have no children to oversee their financial obligations. Was it all too complicated to even consider?

The coffee was excellent, about half consumed when he noticed the flashing lights of a police cruiser following his vehicle.

Barclay pulled to the shoulder and awaited the approach of the officer. Fishing through the glove compartment in search of the ownership and insurance documents, he didn't recognize the officer standing outside the vehicle door.

"Dr. Steadmore! It's me, Jeff Harrington. Where is Faith? You and her are always together. Is everything OK?"

"Jeff, I didn't recognize you in your uniform! I only see you in church services at St. Mary's on Sunday mornings. I know you are the church warden, but I didn't know that you are a police officer.

Faith is fine. She's baking for the coffee hour after Sunday's service. Here is my ownership, driver's licence, and insurance card."

"That won't be necessary Doctor. I didn't recognize you either with those aviator sunglasses and driving cap. I thought perhaps someone had stolen that Mustang you are driving. Mustangs are top choices for car thieves. I ran the licence plate number through my computer and it came back registered to Barclay Steadmore. I didn't expect it to be you out here in the country all by yourself!"

"Jeff, I have a lot on my mind this morning. Have you had your break yet today? There is a little restaurant about a mile or so ahead. Do you have time to have a coffee and I'll fill you in on something I may need some help with?"

Constable Jeff followed Barclay to the restaurant and they both pulled up and parked next to one another. Jeff radioed in that he was on a break and the two sat down at a table for two, both ordering coffee and pie.

It was good to be able to talk to a trusted church member, especially a church warden. Barclay outlined his concerns about leaving for the twelve-month term. Who would look after the condo and the Mustang? Who would oversee payment of bills, and so forth?

Jeff listened and smiled.

"I'd be happy to do all that for you, Doctor. I think that you and Faith ought to go. You have so much experience in ministry that needs to be shared with fellow Christians. You appear to be in good health, as does Faith. If God is calling, you can be assured that He has a mission task that only you two can perform. I say, go for it!"

Their continuing conversation was interrupted by a call coming in over Jeff's vest radio: "There has been a collision on the round-about just outside the town limits. Proceed to investigate."

Constable Jeff abruptly rose to his feet and reached to pick up the bill. Barclay beat him to it and retrieved it before the officer could pick it up.

"Jeff, a word of thanks for your time! Go to work and do your duty! I'll fill Faith in on your offer and let you know if we will take you up on your help. It's been great to talk with a trusted fellow Christian."

It only took Barclay twenty-four minutes to return to his condo. He was excited to fill in Faith with his encounter with Constable Jeff.

Chapter Twenty-Seven

BARCLAY Steadmore could be described as a thoughtful being, not given to rash or sudden decisions. Over the years he had come to understand that not all thinking is of the same quality, and that the first step in becoming a wise individual is to get to know oneself. Thinking is not merely a mental exercise, for a thoughtful person realizes that one lives out what one thinks.

Wise people read voraciously, listen to what others have to offer, and accept responsibility for their lives, choices, mistakes, and influence on others. They know that knowledge is not congruent to wisdom. King Solomon in the Old Testament chose God's gift of wisdom over more knowledge!

While knowing himself, Barclay valued Faith's input into whether or not he should consider Bishop Soulman's offer of that twelve-month assignment in Nigeria. They were open and honest with each other as to how such a mission would affect their lives. What would be Faith's role in the mission? What would be the financial implications in doing so? Would there be adequate medical resources available if one or both should require medical treatment so far away from North America? Was God truly calling them, both of them, into His work?

After two days of engaged conversations and committing the entire concept to prayer, they mutually agreed that it would be best to arrange an appointment with Bishop Soulman to have some of their concerns clarified.

Barclay e-mailed Bishop Soulman's Diocesan Archdeacon and was granted an interview with the Bishop in two weeks, at 2:30 p.m. on a Friday afternoon. Bishop Soulman was currently out of the country meeting with fellow Bishops in the UK.

"At the very least, we will be able to have some of our concerns addressed, Faith. Besides, we always love to have an excuse to return to Tangleville!"

* * *

Barclay and Fr. Joseph had each received an e-mail on Thursday from Fr. David, requesting their permission to allow his two parish members, the electrical engineer and the computer science expert, to join the three clerics at the next regular Friday morning coffee gathering. Both clerics were eager to meet the two volunteers who had agreed to be key people in the design and production of the proposed Abortion Clock.

Barclay was up early on Friday. He showered, shaved, dressed, and ate breakfast, eager for the coffee gathering.

When Barclay arrived, Fr. Joseph was just pulling into the parking lot. Upon entering the coffee shop, they discovered that Fr. David and the two experts were already seated around a table for six. The three rose to their feet, Fr. David making the introductions.

"Fr. Joseph, Dr. Steadmore, meet Peter Stephanopoulos, engineer, and John Adamos, computer whiz."

Firm handshakes were extended by the newly introduced. Fr. Joseph and Dr. Steadmore proceeded to pick up their coffee, the other three already halfway through their first cups.

Fr. David soon steered the conversation into a business mode.

"I've brought along Peter and John today because they have already made some progress in the design and proposed usage of our clock. They now have some questions that need to be addressed ASAP. Fellows, the floor is yours!"

Peter, the engineer began. "We both think that the design of the device needs to be settled first. The object must be portable and easily moved to new locations. That's primary! It must be self-contained, power-wise, perhaps partly solar powered as well as having the capability to be plugged into a standard electrical outlet for extended lengths of time. Solar power will work for short intervals, but it would be advisable to have a battery back-up.

"There are, however, two issues that we must decide upon today. How large do you want the device to be? Give us some guidelines as to its length, height, width and shape. And number two—what do you want it to be capable of displaying? John, this is your bailiwick. You are the computer designer and programmer."

John was eager to jump in.

. "Do you expect the device to only state statistics, for example, the number of abortions per day—let's say—in Canada and the United States? Should it show the total of all abortions in the last ten to twenty years? We have lots of choices in this area. Do you want the screen to first show questions before the stats are given? For example, 'What is the average development of the fetus at the time of the operation?' Or, 'How easy is it for a prospective mother to have the procedure?'

Do you want the screen to be in colour? Should the device be vocal, let's say a bell or buzzer sounds every time a fetus is annihilated? How often do you expect the device to be updated?"

Peter continued, "Does the device itself need some kind of protective outside shell so that it cannot be easily defaced or damaged by pro-choice radicals? All of our questions are doable. Of course, the final cost of the device depends on how simple or complex you want it to be."

Barclay was the first to respond: "Yes, yes, yes, to answer all your questions. We want the device to be educational, eye-catching, particularly of interest to the younger generations who are familiar and experienced with interactive devices. Statistics are mandatory, providing people with the truth about abortion facts in our secular society. But the secular, pro-choice crowd is not interested in facts alone. They are more concerned with the arguments of a mother's rights and a mother's autonomy ... not swayed by arguments of religious morality and not at all moved by accusations of barbarism and extreme bullying when adults so-called rights trump those of the unborn human. We, as priests, know that morality cannot be legislated. What we want to accomplish through the device is the possibility of convincing those who have not yet had to contemplate abortion to never consider one. Thus, the device must be primarily informative, as I said, factual, and arousing curiosity so that people will stop and pay attention. Facts with questions is the way to go."

Fr. Joseph was eager to agree. "Everyone is familiar with large screen televisions. The device ought to be large ... visible and somewhat legible from a distance. The idea, of course, is to get people to pause in what they are doing to read the display. The pro-choice crowd has succeeded in making abortion a ho-hum topic in our age. We want to reverse that attitude."

"Do the answers help you out fellows?" queried Fr. David. "Do you need more input to proceed? I myself would like to see a beating heart design somewhere on the screen momentarily stop every time an abortion takes place. Nothing said … just an indication that a human being has ceased to exist."

"What do you think, John? Do we have enough information to begin the project?" asked Peter.

"Yes! I think we can go back to the drawing board to prepare plans. Why don't we agree to meet in a week's time with a rough design and outline of questions we may wish to flash on the screen before the reader?"

"One other thing, fellows. Do we need to have a name for the device? I've been trying to come up with one now for over a week with no success," admitted Fr. David. "Let's all give it some thought over the next week and be prepared to suggest possible names for the device. It has to be catchy … one that will make people ask, 'What is it?'"

Barclay thanked John and Peter for their input to date saying, "We couldn't do it without you. Next week, we buy the coffee and the crumpets."

"A very productive morning," thought Barclay as he pushed the starter button on the Mustang. "We are on our way to perhaps making a dent in modern society's latest form of slavery … ownership of a developing human being whose life depends solely on the will of the mother to let it live or die. Is death in the womb secular society's extreme practice of bullying? It will be interesting to see how viewers of the Clock will respond to its invasion in the public square."

Chapter Twenty-Eight

It was Thursday, and it had been a week since Barclay sat before his Mac and completed an article for publication in the *Tangleville Mirror*. He was well aware that he had four days before the required deadline to e-mail his next submission.

It was not as if he hadn't been thinking of the subject he wished to address. The topic had been percolating in his mind for at least a month ... the use of the word "progressive." He knew it was time to put the ink to the paper.

WHEN IS PROGRESSIVISM NON-PROGRESSIVE?

Does Father Know Best?

by The Rev. Canon Dr. Barclay Steadmore

There is a word now used over and over again. It is becoming both accepted and applauded: progressivism. It is not a new word. It is merely a corruption of society's once perfectly valid form of thinking: classic liberalism. But progressivism and historic liberalism are not the same thing.

Influenced by the writings of Thomas Hobbes and Adam Smith, a political ideology known as classical liberalism developed in eighteenth century Europe. It extended into nineteenth and twentieth century North America. This ideology stressed the values of the freedom of individuals in many areas of society ... the press, speech, religion, markets, and assembly.

Both classic liberals and conservatives believe that their policies will result in positive outcomes. They are in some ways both on the same side in wanting to better society at large.

Traditional conservatism, especially in politics, is inclined to maintain the existing order ... a philosophy or attitude that is in opposition to rapid change for the sake of change. It promotes gradual reform if not violating long-held respect for traditional institutions. Social change through legislation or publicly funded programs are not to be taken lightly, as though first considering how such programs may conflict with religious views, and freedom of the individual to express non-politically correct speech and promote markets.

However, in recent decades, the label "progressive" has been used to replace classic liberalism, where progressivism, by its current definition, makes progress into ideology.

True liberalism nor conservatism opposes rationality. But unlike liberalism, progressivism is intrinsically opposed to conservatism, inherently hostile to moderation because progress is without qualification good. In the process, tradition is deemed unreasonable, especially in long-held religious and moral values.

Progressivism does not recognize humanity's "fallen state" as outlined in Holy Scripture, but is predicated on the belief of humanity's inevitable rise to godhood! Technology and knowledge will, it is claimed, result in humanity's constant trend towards progress and enlightenment.

But can progressivism be non-progressive? The Christian must consider two questions: Should Christianity convert secular culture, or should secular culture convert Christianity?

In other words, should progressivism trump religion?

Here, neither classic liberalism nor classic conservatism would ever attempt to minimize religious values, beliefs or traditional morality. Progressivism has no qualms in challenging orthodox Christian beliefs and practices.

Where same-sex marriage, abortion, strict sexual mores, Sunday shopping laws, and a host of other

Christian traditions were once held sacrosanct, progressivism considers such conduct as hindering enlightenment.

Thus, Christianity objects! Christianity has always been in favour of true social justice, equality of race, human rights, and relief for the poor, the prisoner and victims of society. But these values are mandated by Holy Scripture and tradition, not invented by government. Christians do not negotiate values!

Faithfulness is a matter of obedience to Christ's teachings and consequently Christians are mandated to convert secular culture. Anything contrary to Holy Scriptures for Christians is non-progressive!

In conclusion, Christians consider secular progressivism as social engineering. "Rethink think," we say, on the present (politically correct) subversive movement that attempts to override freedom of religious convictions through the mechanism of mass government.

For who knows where mass government which does not acknowledge the higher authority of a Creator God will take society? If God is on the sideline, watching, but not involved in humanity's progress, who knows where society may be led? Such is the danger of secular progressivism!

drsteadmore@starmail.com

* * *

When Barclay shut down his Mac, he smiled to himself. "There," he thought. "I've said my peace! Now for the politically correct secular readers to object."

Chapter Twenty-Nine

TWO major events weighed heavily on Barclay's mind: the creation of the not-yet-named Abortion Clock, and Bishop Soulman's invitation to discuss that possible year-long assignment for the Diocese.

Progress was being made on the design for the production of the Abortion Clock. When the two lay experts and the three clerics met on the last Friday of the month, the proposal was approved by everyone!

The machine, for lack of a better word, was to be large, six feet in length, four feet in width and one foot in depth … solar powered with battery and AC back up. On the top was a design of a human heart, about the size of a football, electrically illuminated, pulsating at the same rate as a child's own heart. The device was to be trailer mounted, with stabilizer arms extendable to the ground, so that it could be easily parked or towed in parades.

The machine when activated, would display a warning to its audience:

> Be advised that information displayed may be disturbing, even offensive, to viewers! Abortion Pro-Life viewers will be appalled! Abortion Pro-Choice viewers may object, fearing a backlash, that the information

displayed ought not to be made so easily to the general public. VIEW WITH DISCRETION!

As soon as the warning information would flash off, a sequence of live, minute-by-minute data would follow. First, the number of abortions yearly taking place in Canada ... a ticking digital counter. Each time an additional abortion takes place, the illuminated pulsating heart at the top of the device would fail to flash, indicating that a heart has ceased and the counter would increase by one.

If the viewer continues to watch, a similar format takes place showing the minute-by-minute number of yearly abortions in the US.

Finally, a live counter display would register the number of yearly abortions worldwide.

Following the statistical facts, a series of questions and then answers would flash on the screen, such as:

> What is the average age of a fetus at the time of a typical abortion procedure?
> What do the laws of Canada state pertaining to abortion?
> What does an abortion procedure cost the public health system in Canada?
> Are there limits as to how often a prospective mother may seek an abortion?
> What percentages of abortions are performed to ensure the medical health of the prospective mother, as opposed to a means of desired contraception?

As time advanced, various other questions and answers would be programmed into the machine, ensuring that the device would continually be watched by those whose curiosity was aroused.

The committee was not yet able to agree on a name for the device, but would go ahead with its production ... the name to be added at a later date. One major decision was made: the device must be patented!

There may be financial returns if the device became popular and other communities wished to have their own machine.

Even though the committee, by its own admission, was a pro-life group, it was careful in the question and answer feature of the clock not to say so directly, but to be purely informative. They understood that secular society does not openly discuss abortion in this age, hoping that it does not become a politically divisive issue, which, if the facts were known by a thinking, rational citizenship, new, more restrictive abortion laws may be passed.

Otherwise, out of sight, out of mind!

* * *

Faith and Barclay were up early to make the trip to Tangleville to meet with Bishop Soulman. For the last two weeks they had rehearsed what they were intending to clarify if the Bishop's proposal should sound compelling to accept.

The Bishop had agreed to meet them in the rectory office of St. Timothy's parish. He would be in town to conduct a parish Confirmation service the following Sunday. It would be great to see Fr. Jim Adams again, they both agreed. Fr. Jim, of course, would not be present during the interview, but surely Barclay and Faith would find time during their Tangleville visit to renew old friendships.

On the way, they stopped at the Hi Way Diner, the halfway point, for coffee and a morning dessert. As usual, the "Seat Yourself" sign was there, directing patrons to find an empty table. Just as before, the service was efficient, and without pretence. No small talk on the part of the young lady who took their order. Both were thoroughly impressed with the food and informality of the busy establishment.

They arrived in Tangleville minutes early for their appointment. It gave them a chance to visit the restrooms in the church, tidy up, and prepare to meet the Bishop who was already meeting alone with Fr. Jim in the rector's office. Barclay and Faith were invited to be seated in the waiting room to the left of the secretary's office. Unknown to Barclay and Faith, she was obviously a newly-hired employee since Barclay's retirement from St. Bart's.

They had only been seated for about ten minutes when Fr. Jim and the Bishop emerged from the rector's office. Fr. Jim instantly hurried over to greet Barclay and Faith, a warm handshake for his old clerical friend, and a hug and a kiss for Faith.

"Faith, Doctor, meet Bishop Soulman."

Bishop Soulman first approached Faith, extended his hand in greeting, and firmly shook Barclay's.

"I've heard so much about the two of you. It is wonderful to finally meet you both in person. You have left quite a legacy here in Tangleville. The parish has never stopped reminding me of the good old days of your ministry."

"Thank-you, Bishop. We've wanted to meet you as well, to personally congratulate you on your newly-elected position following Bishop Strictman's retirement. You have constantly been in our prayers."

Five minutes of light conversation followed before Bishop Soulman said goodbye to Fr. Jim, thanking him for the use of his office. He directed Barclay and Faith to sit in two leather-bound chairs in front of the large window looking out onto the parish parking lot.

"Are you driving that red Mustang out there, Canon?" grinned the Bishop.

"Yes! It is in both our names. Faith uses it more than I do. She is great at shifting the six-speed manual transmission."

"I'm a car guy too! I'm picking up a new Chev Camero this coming Monday. It's a convertible as well. Only, mine is black—have to keep it somewhat subdued!"

"So far so good," thought Barclay to himself. "A car enthusiast as well! Already we've made progress."

The Bishop was not a man to mince words, nor to waste valuable time. "What did you two make of my letter I sent to you three weeks ago?"

"Well, to say the least, we were surprized. With me retired, I never expected to be considered for such a position, especially at my age. But, I must say that we were intrigued. We have a number of questions for clarification before we say yes or no."

"Of course, but first let me give you a few more details of the assignment which I did not have the space to outline in my letter."

"Yes, we are anxious for such details. Perhaps more information will illuminate answers to some of our questions."

"The Diocese in Nigeria wants a retired clergy person who holds advanced academic qualifications such as the ones you possess. The one-year position would involve part-time lecturing in their seminary on the subject of practical theology out in the small towns of the Diocese, church growth, media involvement, lay participation in worship, and outreach to non-church people. I think that your media involvement in your former days in Tangleville will be a great asset, especially your writing skills as evidenced by your published articles in the *Tangleville Mirror*."

"Let me continue. The Diocese in Nigeria will provide you, if you accept, with a modern apartment, a small car and fuel, telephone and electrical bills covered. There will be WiFi available in the city, but not in the country regions, and no cell phone service in certain remote areas.

"This is, of course, a part-time position, so you will be expected to work about twenty-five hours per week. The rest of the time is yours. Being a car guy, you will, I suspect, want to do some travelling while over there."

Barclay looked at Faith and caught a quick hint of excitement in her demeanour.

"What about a stipend? Of course, we're living on my pension in this country. I suspect that those payments will still continue and that we will also be covered with a full health care package over there."

"Yes, we can work out that stipend together if you agree to accept the position. When the Diocese over there sends a clergy person here for a year, they are expected to cover expenses from their end."

Faith was eager to have a concern addressed … "Bishop, I have an issue that we need to address. Both Barclay and I are presently in good health. If, by any chance, during the year-long assignment, one of us needs more advanced health care than that third-world medical system can provide, can our assignment, if we say yes, be terminated at our request, allowing us to return home for more advanced medical treatment?"

"That can certainly be written into a contract. Of course!"

The conversation continued with Barclay informing the Bishop that if they were to accept the assignment, that they would need at least four months to set in order certain arrangements for their absence … the renting out of their condo, storage of their car, banking arrangements for the payment of bills, transference of mail, and other matters that would take time to prearrange.

"When do you expect the assignment to get under way?" asked Faith.

"We are somewhat flexible on that date. We can work that out. How does it all sound so far?"

Barclay knew that a yes or a no at this exact moment would be premature. "Can you give us a week to think it over? We may have a few more questions for you."

"I expected that would be the case. I do hope that your answer will be one of acceptance. I'm convinced that you are both perfect for the position."

"Bishop, we will give you a firm answer within a week. We thank you for your confidence in our capabilities and competence to fulfill such an assignment. We certainly will give the matter very serious consideration!"

They were ushered to the foyer and were both embraced by their Bishop. Following brief goodbyes, the Bishop winked at Faith and said, "That Mustang won't mind a year's sabbatical. It may even go up in value if you keep twelve months mileage off the speedometer."

Faith and Barclay grinned. They knew that he wanted a yes within the next few days.

Chapter Thirty

WHILE they were in town, the Steadmores took the Stings out for lunch. It was a lengthy gathering. Harry had a late afternoon appointment chairing the committee he was assigned to oversee by the mayor. The press was to be present and Harry was not looking forward to the event.

Barclay waited for Harry to broach concerns about being a council member, but the topic did not explicitly surface. Between the lines of conversation, Barclay gathered that his friend's enthrallment with being an elected official was waning. Would Harry consider running again in the next municipal election? During the time of their goodbyes, Barclay pressed Harry's hand and assured him that he was always available as a listening ear. "We can meet any time Harry when you need to talk. That's what a friend is for!"

On the return trip to Trinity Harbour, Barclay and Faith discussed the implications of Bishop Soulman's offer. There were so many things to address if the answer was to be yes.

"What is your first response, Faith? Are you leaning one way or another to his request?"

Faith was the driver on the trip to Tangleville, but Barclay took control of the wheel on the return journey. He was always able to do his best thinking, it seemed, while being one with a fine driving automobile.

"If we can work out all the details, and have time to do so, I think I would like the challenge of living in another country, especially in a culture so different from our own. What about you, Bark?"

"I'm leaning that way too, Faith. We are both in good health. With my pension and the yet-to-be-determined stipend we should be able to easily handle the one-year interval. But we really need to look into the medical implications of going … health insurance and the preventative injections for diseases we don't encounter here at home. Then there is banking arrangements and insurance and taxes to be taken care of. How do we make sure that all those things are covered in our absence?"

"Do you think that Constable Harrington really meant it when he offered to take care of everything when he stopped you that day on the road with your top down? He is married, isn't he? They may just be the couple to set our minds at ease if we should agree to go."

They stopped in at the Hi Way Diner for dinner. It was 6:30 p.m. and the parking lot appeared to be full. Barclay dropped Faith at the entrance, while he found a parking spot at the far end of the lot, next to a big red RAM2500 diesel. "Now, there's a truck! I'd love to drive it," mused Barclay. "There is nothing like the sound of a heavy duty diesel at work!"

Faith was already seated at a table for two, awaiting Barclay's entrance. The menus had already been dropped off. Faith had not even perused the options. She had noticed that the special of the day was printed on the bulletin board off to her left: haddock and fries. Barclay ordered the Greek salad and a gyro with extra dressing for the salad.

Their orders, large in size, arrived within ten minutes. "No wonder," remarked Faith, "that the parking lot out there is so crowded. One really gets their monies worth at this place! With so much going to be leftover, guess what you will be having for lunch tomorrow?"

They arrived at their condo at 8:00 p.m. Barclay, as he always did after dinner, checked his e-mails. There was a brief one from Bishop Soulman:

> *So great to meet you both today. I'm really looking forward to a "yes" from each of you. Any more questions or concerns, just get in touch.*
>
> *+ James*

"No wonder he is a Bishop, Faith! I don't think he is the type of person one can say no to easily."

Faith smiled.

* * *

Faith found the Harringtons' telephone number in the church directory and called their home. Marie answered.

"Marie, this is Faith Steadmore calling. We've met briefly at church, but haven't really had an opportunity to know one another. Am I calling at a good time?"

Some small talk continued before Faith centered on the reason for her call.

"Marie, Barclay and I would be delighted if you two would accept our invitation to come for dinner early next week. We usually eat around 6:30 p.m. We have some things that we would like to discuss with you both."

"Faith, we would be happy to accept. Jeff is on afternoon duty every day except Wednesday next week. Would Wednesday work for you?"

"That will be just fine, Marie. Come a little early before we eat to give us some time for conversation. We are looking forward to getting to know both of you better than simply passing the peace at the Sunday Eucharist."

* * *

It was becoming more obvious that both Faith and Barclay were leaning towards accepting Bishop Soulman's offer, providing that their household affairs could be properly addressed while they were away for the year's duration.

Chapter Thirty-One

ACCEPTING the Bishop's offer would mean that Barclay's monthly submissions to the *Tangleville Mirror* would have to cease. Until a possible final date might be decided for leaving Trinity Harbour, he wasn't sure how many more articles he might have time to compose and submit. Certainly if they should agree to say yes to Bishop Soulman's offer, he wanted his final submissions to end in such a fashion that it would theologically tie into all his previous articles … a challenge to his readership.

Sooner or later, whether or not they were leaving, such a final article would eventually be required. In the meantime, he needed to continue work on an article for the next submission, due in three days.

THE SIN OF NO SIN

Does Father Know Best?

by The Rev. Canon Dr. Barclay Steadmore

Imagine one were to stop and ask a stranger on the street the question, "What is sin?" How do you think a modern citizen in the twenty-first century would answer?

Of course the definition of "sin" in today's parlance has taken on many divergent definitions.

Christians, for centuries, have understood "sin" as that which separates us from God, that which is a sacrilege or blasphemy ... anything that is against the will of the Creator. This means that sin has been defined by God, not humans. Thus sin is only forgivable, erased, absolved by a Holy Being.

It has not always been difficult for a person growing up in Christian orders to then define "sin" ... the breaking of the Ten Commandments, not honouring God or giving thanks to Him, not putting God first in one's life, and not loving one's neighbour as oneself. From Biblical principles, theologians have extrapolated the Seven Deadly Sins: lust, gluttony, greed, sloth, wrath, envy, and pride. One of the most hateful sins in the Old Testament Scripture is the worship of idols. In the New Testament, the unforgivable sin is blasphemy against the Holy Spirit. Christians have always experienced no difficulty in identifying sin and its remedy, but times have changed!

Friedrich Nietzsche (1844-1900), the German philosopher, declared: "God is dead." Nietzsche, an atheist, didn't mean that God had actually died, but rather that humanity's idea of God had killed Him. In so stating, society no longer needed to be organized around the idea of divine right to be legitimate, but rather was free to define "sin" in secular terms. Consequently, sin in our modern age is not trespassing the dictates of a Holy God, but instead violating the current notions of what is out of sync with modern thinking. Philosophy and science, it was concluded, were capable of doing that for us.

The death of God didn't result in an entirely good thing. Even Nietzsche was sceptical, for without God, the basic belief system of past generations was in jeopardy. He stated: "When one gives up the Christian faith, one pulls the right to Christian morality out from under one's feet. This morality is by no means self-evident ... Christianity is a system, a whole view of things thought out together. By breaking one main concept out of it, the faith in God, one breaks the whole" (Twilight of the Idols).

Currently, in our modern secular age, "sin" is defined as what we choose sin to be ... short term or long reaching.

On October 22, 1925, Mahatma Gandhi published a list he called "The Seven Social Sins" in his weekly newspaper, *Young India*: "politics without principles, wealth without work, pleasure without conscience, knowledge without character, commerce without morality, science without humanity, worship without sacrifice."

Gandhi was slightly ahead of our time in his publication! But to his list, our age has added: destroying the environment, genetic manipulation, obscene wealth, drug trafficking, creating poverty, violation of human rights, and political correctness.

Christians do not deny the validity of many modern social sins on such lists. What Christians argue is that these sins are the direct consequences of Nietzsche's "God is dead" pronouncement ... that these so defined "sins" are self-inflicted when God is abandoned.

Christians argue and believe that God exists! Thus, humanity's rejection of God, if God exists, may be deemed as a major moral trespass: The Sin of No Sin. God must not be amused!

Without the existence of God, secular society defines our sins, solves our sins, and grants absolution of sins—no need for God's action!

One amusing result occurs. Christians remind secular society that if God does not exist, then it is impossible to curse. Webster's Dictionary defines a curse as "a prayer or wish for harm to come to someone or something." If there is no God, why would anyone pray? Why state the words "by God" if there is no God? It would make more sense to curse saying "by Jupiter," or "by Venus," or "by Chevrolet." But who would be offended if you did? One would not expect the same objection that might be anticipated from a Christian who objects to using the Lord's name in vain.

I challenge my readers to invent a swear word, that if God is dead, would offend anyone. Maybe the "God is dead" philosophy does result in a positive but short-sighted consequence not first anticipated. Ha!

One closing observation, a question to consider: If God is dead, and the Sin of No Sin is not taken seriously, what would be a list of possible new sins for future humankind to invent? And who would consider taking sins seriously defined by human conscience when compared to taking zealously violating sin as defined by a Holy God?

Barclay was smiling!

God help us!

drsteadmore@starmail.com

Chapter Thirty-Two

"**BARCLAY,** have you forgotten that the Harringtons are coming for dinner this evening? Have you made a list of the items you wish to discuss with them before we decide how to answer Bishop Soulman's invitation?"

Barclay was way ahead of her this time!

"Faith, I've been working on that list now for three days. It just seems to be getting longer and longer. I'm really looking forward to their visit. What are you planning to serve for dinner?"

"I'm serving roast beef, baked potatoes, squash, and cauliflower. Dessert will be apple pie and ice cream. How does that sound?"

"What if one of them does not like either of your vegetable choices? Maybe it would be a good idea to have peas or corn ready as well!"

"What you are saying is that you yourself can't stand cauliflower, right? OK, I'll have another vegetable ready as well."

Barclay was proud of himself. After all those years of marriage, he had finally learned to be more diplomatic than in the early years of matrimony.

Faith was on to him! "Bark, you didn't fool me. I know your old tricks! But, in spite of them, I love you!"

The Harringtons arrived fifteen minutes before the 6:30 hour. Marie was carrying a lovely bouquet of cut flowers, which Faith immediately arranged in an attractive water-filled vase and placed on the mantle of the fireplace.

Barclay and Jeff proceeded to the den while Faith gave Marie a quick tour of the Steadmore condo. It was obvious that the two were quickly becoming at ease with one another. Following the short tour, Marie joined the men in their conversation.

Twenty minutes passed before Faith called everyone to the dining room table. Barclay gave the blessing for the meal. Everyone had joined hands for the occasion and each crossed themselves at the Amen.

Barclay served the plates, asking who would prefer the meat well done or rare. Both Marie and Jeff chose the squash and cauliflower. Faith glanced over at Barclay and gave him a quick wink. Only Barclay chose the corn and squash.

After the dessert and coffee, everyone quickly helped Faith clear the dishes, loaded them into the dishwasher, and all four retired to the den, fresh coffee in their cups. It was so pleasing to see how easily the guests were fitting into a comfortable relationship with their hosts. Finally Barclay opened up the conversation with details of Bishop Soulman's offer of the one-year position in Nigeria.

"Jeff, I've already given you some details of our hesitation in saying yes to the Bishop, that day you stopped me in the Mustang out in the country. Marie, I told Jeff that Faith and I would feel more positive in accepting his offer if we knew that a number of concerns had been put aside before we say yes."

"Barclay, Jeff filled me in on your conversation that evening after his shift. But let's go over the items that both of you are concerned about. I think that Jeff and I may be able to solve some of the issues at stake."

"Since I spoke with Jeff, Faith and I have worked out some of the details of being absent for a year. We both agree that we don't want to sell or rent our condo. It's paid for in full. All we would need to look after financially are taxes, insurance, condo fees, and utility bills. Those could be paid through automatic bank withdrawals just as we do now. But, we would have to have the place inspected on a regular basis to keep the insurance policy valid. You know … check for water leaks, sewer back-up, and so forth.

"Also, I don't want to put the Mustang up for sale. It is a collector car and keeps going up in value year by year. But, it needs to be started and driven once in a while to keep it lubricated. We have a garage, but it is not just anyone that I would trust to take it out on the road."

"Then there is always the risk of a break and enter, and not being home to report it. The insurance company and the police would not be made aware of the incident," added Faith.

Marie and Jeff were smiling!

"Jeff is a cop and I'm an insurance adjuster. Who would be better to leave the keys with than us?" responded Marie.

That response was exactly what Faith and Barclay needed to hear. Their conversation extended for another three-quarter hours, with Barclay suggesting that he and Faith open a bank account in the Harringtons' names to provide for unexpected expenses beyond the normal monthly withdrawals. The Harringtons would then be able to pay for any repairs and so forth that may arise without having to contact Africa for permission.

Jeff cautiously broached the subject. "Do you two have an up-to-date will? You have no children who normally would be called into action in case of ill health or other unexpected circumstances which might render one or both of you incapable of conducting your affairs."

"We do Jeff, but it hasn't been updated in some time. Great advice! Faith and I will make an appointment with our lawyer … update everything, and give you and Marie a copy with the names, addresses, and contact information so that you can be in the loop. We hope it will not be necessary for such emergencies, but it is better that we are prepared than not."

None of the four wanted the evening to end. It was clear that Barclay and Faith were getting closer than ever to finally saying yes to Bishop Soulman.

Jeff and Marie finally excused themselves at 11:15 p.m., thanking their hosts for a wonderful evening. Clearly the two families were to continue their new friendship, regardless of whether or not Barclay and Faith were to accept the offer to leave Trinity Harbour for the year's mission mandate.

Hugs were extended all around, and Faith and Barclay walked the Harringtons to their Camry.

"Be careful, Jeff," advised Barclay. "You never know who is behind the wheel out there this time of night!"

"You're so right, Barclay. But remember, I am a cop who has done many night shifts. I know the signs of distracted or impaired drivers. Give us a call when you have reached a decision."

Barclay and Faith returned to the den, unable to unwind after a most enjoyable evening. They sat up to talk, not yet ready to turn in for the night.

After twenty minutes of rehearsing a postmortem on the evening, Barclay was ready to ask the question.

"What do you think, Faith? Are you any closer to an answer for Bishop Soulman?"

"I say, let's go for it! How about you?"

"I think that the Harringtons have put my mind at ease. I don't know how we can say no to the Bishop. Let's send him an e-mail in the morning, with a 'yes' answer, requesting the date he would like us to depart. What say we try to encourage him to give us about a four month lead time to get ready to go?"

"I'm with you, dear. The Lord is opening doors! I think that we would be wrong to say that we wouldn't pass through them. I'm tired, I'm going to turn in."

They exchanged a kiss and Barclay replied, "I'll be there in a few minutes. I think that there is still one piece of that apple pie in the fridge."

Chapter Thirty-Three

AFTER breakfast the following morning, Barclay composed a brief e-mail to Bishop Soulman advising him that he and Faith were in agreement of accepting the one-year appointment to the Nigerian Diocese. A request was made for a four month preparation time to prepare for the departure date, as well as detailed information on the job description of the assignment.

Within twenty minutes, Bishop Soulman e-mailed Barclay:

Dear Barclay and Faith:

I am absolutely delighted that you are accepting the position! The two of you are perfectly suited for the task. I have informed the Diocesan Archdeacon and asked that he forward to you a detailed job description. Of course, you and Faith will need to meet with him several times in the near future to work out the stipend, insurance requirements, medical requirements, flight arrangements, and so forth for your visit. You will be hearing from him shortly.

One more requirement—you will need to be ready to depart in three months. Your request for four is simply beyond what the Nigerian Bishop requires. I do hope that you and Faith can work around such a tight timetable.

Again, my thanks and best wishes!
+ James

"Faith, I've just heard from the Bishop. He has given us three months to prepare for departure. Do you think that we can get everything in order in such a short time?"

"We have no choice, do we? We will make it work."

* * *

Bishop Soulman's e-mail set in motion a series of procedures to be completed before their departure. The two of them drew up a list of things which would need to be attended to before their flight. The closing of their condo and the storage of the Mustang would be taken care of by the Harringtons. Jeff and Marie would check into their residence at least once a week and Jeff smiled when he said that he would be sure to take the Mustang for a run every few weeks, just to keep it "ready" for the Steadmores' return.

There were two major items to be addressed: a meeting with their lawyer to update their wills, and a final submission to the *Tangleville Mirror*. Barclay wanted his final publication to be an all-encompassing article to tie together the previous ones. He was certain that it would require more time to compose than any of his previous submissions.

"Barclay, I think that we ought to make a trip to Tangleville before we leave and visit the Stings. Let's set up a weekend to do so and spend one last Sunday at St. Bart's. There are a number of parishioners to whom we need to say our goodbyes."

"Let's do it near the end of next month. I'm going to need to spend a lot of time before my Mac and with the two priests and lay members working on the Abortion Clock plans. Go ahead and see how our timetable for the visit can fit into the Stings' plans."

* * *

Barclay decided to compose a letter of resignation to the *Tangleville Mirror*. It had been agreed upon at the time of his acceptance to write twice monthly articles, where either party, the *Mirror* or himself, could cancel the contract with a two week notification.

Mr. James Parker, Editor
The Tangleville Mirror
197 Main Street
Tangleville, ON K3J 1B1

Dear Mr. Parker:

I begin by expressing how enjoyable our working relationship has been for the past two years. I commend you and Samantha Birkley for publishing each of my submissions without editorial intervention. You have kept your word and I believe that I have been open and fair in how I have expressed my views on a broad array of published topics. Thank-you!

My spouse Faith and I have accepted an offer made to us by our Bishop James Soulman to travel to Nigeria for a one-year assignment. Consequently, I am hereby submitting my resignation effective in two weeks following your receipt of this letter. I will be submitting one more article for publication, which is intended to be the conclusion of previous articles.

Again, I must express how grateful I am for having been permitted to be a contributing writer to your newspaper.

God's richest Blessing,

Barclay+

The Rev. Canon Dr. Barclay Steadmore

Barclay walked with Faith to the Post Office and dispatched his letter of resignation by registered mail to James Parker.

"Faith, that is one more item off our list! It is becoming clearer in my mind that a big change is coming in our lives! How about a coffee at the Sip and Savour Bake Shop?"

"I'm on! I didn't bring my purse. Are you up to picking up the tab?"

"I have a $5 bill in my pocket. So don't sip large on my generosity," grinned Barclay.

Faith squeezed his hand, but said nothing.

Chapter Thirty-Four

BEING Friday, Barclay prepared to meet his retired cleric friends for coffee.

The last one of the three to arrive was always teased by the other two. "Getting a little tired, are you Steadmore? Can't quite keep up the pace you once enjoyed?" quipped Fr. David.

"I thought that if I arrived last, you fellows might have purchased my coffee. See you didn't do that though!"

"You know the rules, Father. 'The last shall be first.' So, we will have our usual." They knew that the Lord didn't mean it that way, but were having a little fun with their brother.

Barclay proceeded to the counter, and smiling to himself, ordered the coffee and muffin treats for the three of them. "Just wait until I tell them of our plans to go to Nigeria. That will end my always picking up the tab!"

Their conversations always seemed to follow a similar pattern … what had taken place in each other's lives over the past seven days … a discussion surrounding news from each other's denomination … family and friends' health concerns, the weather.

Finally, Barclay broke the news of him and Faith accepting the year-long assignment in Africa. Fr. David and Fr. Joseph were intrigued and eager for more pertinent details.

Over a second cup of coffee all around, Barclay filled in some of the details of the assignment ... the last item to be outlined was the departure date.

"The Bishop has told us to be ready in three months. That really puts us in a bit of a state of panic, but we will make it! What I am really going to miss, I think, is the day our Abortion Clock hits the streets. I really wanted to be an observer of the public's reaction to its debut. Has there been any information, Fr. David, as to when that date may be?"

"Barclay, it is going to be touch and go for you. The committee has informed me that they are making great progress. The electronics have been sorted out and the physical design finalized. I'm told that it is possible that it can be ready for our viewing and final OK in about two months. You may get to see it yet before you and Faith depart."

"Have we decided on a name for the device?" inquired Barclay.

"No we haven't," replied Fr. Joseph. "I've been pondering what it should be called. The more I think about it, I am convinced that the word 'abortion' should not appear in its title display. The word is just too divisive ... too polarizing in our modern age. Some people, if they were to immediately guess what might follow ... an anti-abortion pro-life message ... may refuse to pause, to continue to pay attention to the statistical data to follow.

"That would defeat the purpose of our project. What we really want the device to do is to arouse spectators' curiosity, to entice observers into wanting to see what is going to be revealed. It is to be an educational device. After all, it is to be factual, if you will."

Fr. Joseph continued, "We want the ill-informed to be appalled at what is taking place in our modern age ... dismayed to the point where some form of collective action may be taken to eventually end such medical procedures."

"I think that you are right on, Joseph. For the average person on the street, abortion is just a word ... not reality! Of course, the pro-choice group, when they figure out the device, may wake up our sleeping, complacent population, and will be doing everything in their power to prohibit its public presence. You are right, Joseph. The title on the device must not immediately give away its intent."

"Perhaps, a title something like 'The Truth May Set Them Free,' or 'Just so You Will Know' will spark the observer to take time to digest the entire message on the screen. Some kind of title that doesn't immediately divulge what is to follow!" added Fr. David.

"Curiosity before shutting down one's mind," summarized Barclay.

"Well, we have time yet to decide," reminded Fr. David. "Right now, let's allow the design experts to put a working device together, and hopefully Barclay will be able to see it in action before it hits the public."

All three agreed to work on a suitable name to be emblazoned on the final production model.

It was a most productive morning coffee meeting for the three friends. Barclay was determined that he wouldn't be last to arrive at the next Friday meeting.

* * *

Faith and Barclay seemed to have a thousand little projects to address, which made the weeks pass quickly prior to their upcoming trip.

They set up a meeting with their bank to make sure that each of their routine monthly bills would be automatically paid from their combined savings and chequing accounts. Their insurance company was contacted to inform the representative that their condo would be routinely checked while they were away, giving the company the names and contact information for Jeff and Marie Harrington.

Barclay took the Mustang to his local auto mechanic to have the oil and filter changed, tires checked, and all the fluids topped up for the year's storage.

The Harringtons and the Steadmores routinely met at church on Sunday mornings, and every two weeks, Barclay and Faith took their new friends to dinner at a local restaurant, each time keeping them informed of every step made for their departure. Each time they met, Barclay and Faith were growing increasingly more confident that all was going to be in good hands. The anxiety level of being away was lessening week by week.

Jeff and Marie agreed to pick up their mail that would arrive at the condo, sort it, and forward pieces that appeared to be either personal or urgent to the Steadmores' new address in Nigeria … their address yet unknown. All four of them were computer savvy, so keeping in touch would be quick and easy.

Chapter Thirty-Five

The Steadmores were looking forward to one last trip to Tangleville before they were to leave the country. Faith arranged reservations for two nights, Friday and Saturday, at a new motel in town, the Your Sweet Dreams Inn, after contacting Annie to advise that they were going to be in Tangleville for the three days.

Annie, of course tried to persuade their good friends to bunk in at the Stings. But Faith was not willing to let them go to the extra work of preparing for guests. They agreed to join the Stings at home for dinner on the Friday evening, but the Stings would be the guests of the Steadmores on Saturday evening at a local steak house.

"Bark, let's leave around 11:00 a.m. and stop at our favourite halfway spot for lunch. You know, the Hi Way Diner. It will be at least a year or more before we will again be visiting the Stings."

They arrived at the Your Sweet Dreams Inn around 3:30 p.m. and after checking in, Barclay decided to take an hour's nap before preparing to dress to visit the Stings. Faith left him behind and drove to the Tangleville Mall. A favourite dress store was her intended destination. Barclay slept soundly until her return at 5:15 p.m.

Following a quick shower, Barclay dressed and was ready to head out for their visit with the Stings. Faith applied fresh makeup, fixed her hair, and the two were off. They were excited to greet their old friends once again.

It was like old times! Hugs all around! Annie had prepared another of her famous roast beef dinners, served with Yorkshire Pudding. Dessert was apple crisp, made from scratch.

After dinner, with second cups of coffee in hand, all four retired to the large family room, a fire blazing in the fireplace. It was as if the couples had never separated a few years before when the Steadmores moved to Trinity Harbour. Good friends are forever!

Faith and Barclay brought Annie and Harry up to date on their assignment in Nigeria, now only three weeks away to their departure date.

Harry was concerned for their safety while abroad, but Faith assured them that if it was God's will that they should go, they would be in good hands all around.

"What about your condo?" inquired Annie. "Who is looking into it while you are away?"

Barclay explained their connection to the Harringtons, who had agreed to look after such details, including taking the Mustang for warm-ups every few weeks.

Annie smiled, always the car guy. "Look after it! If the Harringtons can't find the time to keep it from getting used to retirement, I'll gladly make a trip to Trinity Harbour and exercise it myself!"

Harry didn't quite get it! A car was only a car, as far as he was concerned. But he didn't argue with Annie. After all, she was far more in tune with fine automobile ownership than he was. For she drove that

Jag XKE convertible! Barclay couldn't afford such a valuable collector car as she possessed, but both were automobile enthusiasts. Those who don't possess such devotion to driving, simply don't get it!

When the opportunity permitted, Barclay raised the topic that he hoped would be looked upon favourably by Annie and Harry ... the need for two executors to discharge their wills in the event that he and Faith should somehow not be able to make it back home alive.

He explained how chances were slim for such an unforeseen event, however, since he and Faith had neither children nor close relatives, they considered Annie and Harry their closest and most trusted friends.

It was clear that Annie and Harry were moved and honoured to readily answer yes.

"What about Power of Attorney documents to oversee health and financial matters in case both of you, heaven forbid, should reach a time when you are incapable of attending to such matters?"

"Harry, those were our next concerns. We were hoping that you would accept our first request, and then we were going to address your last concerns. Will you and Annie also fulfil those roles in the event that Faith or I can't do so for each other?"

Annie and Harry rose to their feet and with arms outstretched, advanced towards Faith and Barclay ... warm hugs as tears of friendship flowed all around.

"Cicero, in *De Amicitia*, is quoted as saying, 'A friend is, as it were, a second self,'" thought Barclay. "

George Herbert certainly was correct when he wrote in *Jacula Prudentum*, 'When a friend asks, there is no tomorrow.'"

"Harry, Annie ... when Faith and I get back to Trinity Harbour, we are going to visit our lawyer and have our documents brought up to date. We certainly can't thank you enough for agreeing to accept those positions. There are no others we love and trust as you two!"

It was getting late, and Faith and Barclay finally rose to retire to their motel. Harry and Annie walked them to their car and once again embraced their guests.

"Look after that Mustang, Doctor," teased Annie. "Someday it may be a classic!"

* * *

On Saturday, Faith and Barclay slept in later than usual, and when 11:00 a.m. arrived, they went out for brunch at one of Tangleville's better known restaurants, Grandma's Kitchen.

"Drop me off at the mall, Bark. I know that you want to stop in at St. Bart's to visit Canon Matthew. He usually is there on a Saturday, getting ready for a wedding or Sunday services. If he is not there, you will no doubt put the top down and take a run out into the country. I'll call when I'm ready to be picked up."

Canon Matthew's SUV was in the rector's parking spot, so Barclay drove over to a coffee shop, picked up a couple of critters and coffee, and surprized Canon Matthew, who was alone in the church. He was working behind his office desk. He was overjoyed to greet Barclay and the two settled in for a half-hour conversation. Matthew had a wedding to prepare for at 3:00 p.m., so Barclay said he would see him tomorrow at the 10:30 a.m. service. The sun was shining; it was 24 degrees Celsius. The top was lowered and Barclay headed out of town for an afternoon cruise.

"I wonder how Harry is making out in his role as the town councillor. The last time we talked about it, he was wrestling with being true to himself and yet fulfilling the expected role of his electors. I'll somehow get around to finding out tonight at dinner," he thought.

The warm wind and sunshine allowed him to become one with the joy of rural, top-down driving.

* * *

The Stings and the Steadmores met at 6:30 p.m. at Lucy's Steak and Chop House, which was new to Tangleville. It seemed as if their dinner conversation from the previous night easily continued.

It didn't take long for Harry to get around to telling Faith and Barclay that he was planning on re-running for his council seat in the next town elections. It was obvious to Barclay that Harry had found new confidence in himself in his present role as councillor … able to stand up for his moral convictions in the voting procedures that arose. It was welcomed news!

The four lingered longer than expected at their table, over second orders of coffee and desserts. No one wanted the evening to end for all four knew that it would be at least a year's duration before their next meal together.

They left the restaurant at 10:30 p.m., Barclay picking up the bill.

Saying their goodbyes in the parking lot, both couples promised to remember each other in their prayers, and continue to regularly keep in touch by e-mail.

"If you need anything, Faith and Barclay, during your stay in Nigeria, just ask. I'll be there for you," reassured Annie. Both Harry and Faith knew that her statement involved money if they should unexpectedly need it. Annie, ever the generous and forbearing Christian!

On Sunday morning, the Steadmores set out early after a quick breakfast at McDonald's to return to Trinity Harbour. There were still so many things to tidy up in the short three-week period before their departure.

Chapter Thirty-Six

So many last things to attend to ... so little time remaining!

Faith and Barclay set up an appointment with their lawyer and brought their wills up to date, with the Stings acting as executors and having power of attorney over financial, property, and personal care matters. At the lawyer's suggestion, they added a clause in each of their wills directing that, in case of death, all their assets were to be liquidated into a benevolent fund, overseen by the Stings.

At the appointment with their local bank, they made provisions for funds to be easily transferred to an account to be opened on their arrival in Nigeria. The bank was authorized to automatically withdraw payments for all bills over the next twelve-month period related to taxes, hydro, water, telephone, computer services, and insurance policies.

A safety deposit box was rented and Faith and Barclay stored items they didn't wish to take with them ... jewellery, dress watches, personal medical information, and a copy of their updated legal documents. Extra keys to their condo and Mustang were also included.

They decided that all mail during their absence was to be delivered to their condo. As previously agreed, the Harringtons would sort it and what was not to be discarded would be sent to Africa every two weeks. Keeping in touch regularly by e-mail, it would be easy for Marie and Jeff to determine what was relevant to send and what was merely junk mail. With the mail being delivered daily, it would make it appear that their condo was being lived in and not vacant. The Mustang would continue to be parked in the underground parking lot. Of course, Barclay would be taking his Mac laptop with him to their new African residence.

Over the years, Barclay and Faith could never agree on the value of insurance policies, with Faith maintaining that a minimum amount of coverage to cover their final death expenses was all that was necessary. Barclay always wanted to purchase larger amounts of insurance to make sure that if he were to pass before her, Faith would be financially secure. It was the one topic that was always causing friction in their marriage.

Without telling Faith, Barclay purchased extra travel health insurance for their one-year absence, and two large accidental death policies ... each valued at $1,000,000. Accidental death policies are very inexpensive, for the risk of accidental death is very low. He reasoned that he would inform Faith of these two purchases after they arrived in Nigeria.

There was one major task left for Barclay to complete ... his final submission to the *Tangleville Mirror*. He had been mulling over its content for some time, wanting the final article to, in some way, be a personal challenge for his readership, both to those who were his fans and those who were his critics. He finally settled on the title!

UNTANGLING ONE'S LIFE

Does Father Know Best?

by The Rev. Canon Dr. Barclay Steadmore

As my final submission to the *Tangleville Mirror*, after previously commenting on many contemporary issues, I want this article to take a different direction. Instead of focusing on topics that some readers may say, "These issues don't apply to me," this final editorial will. A rational individual would be foolish not to do a personal inventory.

Two questions: Do you know who you are and what you believe, and do you stand up for your convictions and own them?

Dr. Jordan Peterson, the clinical psychologist from the University of Toronto, in his best selling book *12 Rules for Life: An Antidote to Chaos*, formulates principles to help one address these two questions.

He states: "To stand up straight with your shoulders back is to accept the terrible responsibility of life, with eyes wide open" (27).

Now hang on to those two words: terrible responsibility.

On page 159, he summarizes: "set your house in perfect order before you criticize the world." He uses a metaphor to drive home this statement. I paraphrase his admonition: clean up your own room before you attempt to clean up the world.

He then adds that in so doing, "you will untangle your past" (158).

Dr. Peterson's words are precisely applicable to modern contemporary secular society. Life is a "terrible responsibility" in so many aspects of trying to make sense of who one is and how one fits into modern living. Of course, he is speaking in psychological parlance. So many are not sure of what they believe and how they should react to the confusing forces around them. As a result, it is easy to sit on the fence, so to speak, and simply let the world pass by …

As a theologian, I have observed that when it comes to matters of faith and doctrinal belief, fence sitting is all too common. For if there is a God, a God who will hold individuals accountable to Him, then, as Dr. Peterson puts it, life is a "terrible responsibility." One's eternal salvation is at stake!

Now if you gamble that God does not exist, so be it. That is one's human right to decide. (One cannot prove that God exists or prove that he doesn't.) But if one is wrong, the expression "terrible responsibility" becomes even more consequential.

Fence sitting for Christians is not an option. The writer of the Book of Revelation quotes the angel's words to the Church in Laodicea: "I know your works; you are neither cold nor hot. I wish that you were either cold or hot" (Chapter 3:15).

Do you want to untangle your life?

Settle in your thinking whether God exists, or He doesn't. If you decide that He does, then He must become first in your life ... before everything ... before ambition, materialism, power, pursuit of pleasure, fame, and success. In other words, God first, others second, self third!

No fence sitting ... no compromising of principles to go alone with the secular crowd. Focus on what is meaningful and noble in your life.

Of course, such a cross will be heavy to carry, but the rewards of doing so will ensure peace of mind ... as Dr. Peterson puts it in psychological language, an "Antidote to Chaos," and as Jesus puts it in the Gospel of Luke:

"If any want to become my followers, let them deny themselves and take up their cross daily and follow me. For those who want to save their life will lose it, and those who lose their life for my sake will save it" (Chapter 9:23-24).

St. John summarizes:

"I have said these things to you so that my joy may be in you, and that your joy may be complete" (Chapter 15:11).

First, untangle thyself! By so doing, one small step is made in untangling the world.

Shakespeare, in *Hamlet*, said:

"This above all, To thine ownself be true; and it must follow, as the night the day, thou canst not then be false to any man" (1.3.78-80).

drsteadmore@starmail.com

Another era of Barclay's life had ended as he pressed the send key of his Mac to forward the final submission to the *Tangleville Mirror*. In many aspects, it was a bittersweet moment. What a privilege it had been to be a monthly voice to the Tangleville readers.

But now, a new door was opening for Faith and himself. Doors open and doors close. To step through them is always a matter of choice ... a matter of faith. John Galsworthy was right on when he quoted in *Swan Song*, "If you do not think about the future, you cannot have one."

"Surely, God has opened another door for Faith and myself," thought Barclay. "'The future struggles against being mastered,' goes the old Latin proverb. Thank-you God, for the hinges of life!"

* * *

The evening before their departure date from Westwick International Airport, Faith and Barclay had taken the Harringtons out for a goodbye dinner. They turned over the keys to their condo, the Mustang, and their safety deposit box at their local bank. Spirits were high all around. Their departure time was set for 5:40 p.m. the next day.

Faith and Barclay were up early the next morning. They walked to their favourite coffee shop for one last light breakfast before the Harringtons were to arrive to drop them off at the airport.

There were goodbyes all around and warm hugs before Barclay and Faith checked in and received their boarding passes. Barclay, knowing how uncomfortable modern airline seats can be on a long flights, had prepaid for seats next to one of the emergency doors, giving them extra room to stretch their legs out during the first eight-hour leg of the flight.

Settling in after the flight crew had served an inflight dinner, Barclay was getting ready to take a nap. He had always been able to catch a brief shut-eye period regardless of the time of day. Faith was caught up in the second chapter of a novel she had purchased at the airport before takeoff.

"Faith, look out the window. What a glorious sunset! My father used to say, 'Sunset at night, sailor's delight!' I'm looking forward to a radiant morning!"

"Bark, I have a premonition that your dad's saying may have a deeper meaning than you may realize!"

Barclay didn't go there! He simply reached over, gently grasped her hand, and whispered, "I love you."

Epilogue

TWO days following the Steadmore's departure to Nigeria, the following article appeared in the October 23, 2018 issue of the *Tangleville Mirror:*

FLIGHT 791 FROM WESTWICK INTERNATIONAL AIRPORT MISSING

News of the non-arrival of Sunday's Flight 791 on the refuelling stop-over in Europe to Nigeria confirms that all passengers and crew are missing. Search and rescue efforts have located what is believed to be the crash site with no human remains discovered.

It appears that the crash must have been violent, as only broken parts of the exterior of the aircraft were found, along with the emergency exit escape door on the right side of the aircraft.

The *Tangleville Mirror* has learned that two long-time prominent former residents of Tangleville were on board ... The Rev. Canon Dr. Barclay Steadmore, former rector of Tangleville's St. Bartholomew's Anglican Church, and his spouse, Faith. They were on their way to fulfill a one-year assignment to an Anglican Diocese in Nigeria. The members of St. Bartholomew's parish are in shock with grief.

It is certain that the Steadmores were on board, as the flight records indicated that they were assigned seats next to the right-side emergency door. Only one seat was discovered floating on the surface of the Atlantic, the very seat that Dr. Steadmore had been assigned.

What confirms Dr. Steadmore's death was the discovery of his backpack which was tucked under the seat cushion. In the backpack was found his personal diary, with the last entry recorded at 11:32 p.m. the night before the crash. The entry read: "Looking forward to a new dawn."

If that diary was ever to be published, we are certain that it would reveal fascinating personal details of his ministry here in Tangleville.

Staff of the *Tangleville Mirror*, and the residents of the town are mourning the deaths of a beloved priest and his spouse.

* * *

The *Tangleville Mirror* published the following article on December 3, 2018:

LARGE CROWDS GATHER AROUND A NEW DEVICE ON MAIN STREET

Yesterday, a heavy-duty Ford F250 pick-up truck towing a large flatbed trailer carrying a massive attention-getting device resembling a flat-screen TV was unceremoniously parked in front of the Court House on Main Street. The device was active, displaying information and questions before the inquisitive onlookers gathered on the Court House lawn.

No one was present to claim ownership of the truck and trailer. The active device was self-powered and did not contain a title other than a sentence over the top of the screen which read: "THE TRUTH MAY SET THEM FREE" ... words adapted from St. John's Gospel, Chapter 8, verses 31 and 32, which record the words of Jesus: "If you continue in my word, you are truly my disciples, and you will know the truth, and the truth will make you free." The device was certainly catching the attention of the ever-growing curious crowd. As they watched, it became apparent that statistical data on the frequency of therapeutic abortions in Canada, the United States, and the global community was systematically being displayed.

It was soon obvious that the onlookers were slowly but steadily dividing into two camps of observers, which on analysis by our staff, could be labelled as pro-life supporters and pro-choice advocates.

The pro-life crowd was horrified by the frequency of the operations, morally condemning the medical procedure as evil. Pro-choice advocates were dismayed that such information should be made public, claiming that a woman's right to control her body was personal, and no one else's business but her own. Emotions were running high. Questions were being asked by young children: "Mommy, Daddy, what is an abortion?" Some children, already aware of the procedure, quizzed parents: "Did you ever consider aborting me before I was born?" Adults opposed to the procedure were asking one another why they as pro-life supporters are compelled to pay into the public health system to cover the cost of abortions.

The truck and trailer were legally parked. No one showed up to move the vehicle, the trailer or device until three in the afternoon. The driver, when pressed by the media, refused to be interviewed, only to say that the information on the device was factual and intended as a teaching instrument to transmit facts which the secular media has generally buried.

Our news staff has uncovered the origins of the device, which we have simply labelled as an "Abortion Clock."

It turns out that the new controversial device is the brainchild of three retired clerics, Fr. Joseph Murphy, a Roman Catholic priest, Fr. David Antonopoulos, of the Orthodox Church, both living in Trinity Harbour, and our own, now deceased, Dr. Barclay Steadmore, former rector of St. Bartholomew's Anglican parish here in town. They have patented the instrument and decided to first test it out here in our town.

The genius of the device is that it doesn't officially take sides in the abortion debate, but only transmits facts ... information to invite discussion between opposing groups and encourage dialogue on the subject. It is silent ... will not shout down objectors. One cannot argue with a machine. However, since its inventors are clerics, it is reasonable to conclude that the three priests were pro-life advocates.

The *Tangleville Mirror* has since learned that many church denominations in Tangleville have signed up to display the device on their church parking lots. Demand for the production of more such devices has prompted the designers of the device to mass produce the device for display purposes in other nearby towns.

For anyone yet puzzled by the title on the device, "The Truth May Set Them Free," it becomes abundantly clear that the "them" in the sentence is meant to be interpreted as the "victims" of abortion.

The *Mirror* is predicting that secular society has not heard the end of the ever-dividing abortion debate. We are not surprised that even in death, the voice of influence of The Rev. Canon Dr. Steadmore has been resurrected!

Donald H. Hull, D. Min.

Previous titles in this series:

Tangleville, Just About Any Town Anywhere

Untangling Tangleville, Stepping Out! Just as Any Town Can

Printed in Canada